american
stranger

Also by David Plante

FICTION

Slides
Relatives
The Age of Terror
The Catholic
The Family
ABC
The Accident
The Country
The Foreigner
The Woods
Annunciation

NONFICTION

The Ghost of Henry James
The Darkness of the Body
Figures in Bright Air
Difficult Women
My Mother's Pearl Necklace
The Native
Prayer
American Ghosts
The Pure Lover
Becoming a Londoner : A Diary
Worlds Apart

american stranger

a novel

david plante

delphinium books

AMERICAN STRANGER

Copyright © 2018 by David Plante

Library of Congress Cataloguing-in-Publication Data is available on request.

ISBN 978-1-88-328573-9

18 19 20 21 22 RRD 10 9 8 7 6 5 4 3 2 1

First Edition

Jacket and interior design by Greg Mortimer

I . . . am amazed by the horrible homelessness all

French-Canadians in America have. . . .

—Jack Kerouac

one

Alone in her parents' Manhattan apartment, Nancy walked around naked. Closed up for the month of August while she and her parents had been in Amagansett, the apartment was still and dim and hot, the dark green, old-fashioned blinds pulled almost all the way down to the windowsills.

She raised a blind and looked out over the traffic on Fifth Avenue and the massed trees of the park beyond, then she turned to look about the living room as if for someone who might be there. The living room appeared enormous to her. The parquet floor was bare, the rugs rolled up and pushed against a wall. Arranged at right angles to the sofa and armchairs were two Biedermeier chairs and a Biedermeier table, their delicate legs reflected in the highly polished floor, and at the end of the room was a tall, narrow Biedermeier cabinet, of cherrywood with ebony rosette inlays along a pediment held by two thin ebony columns, this piece of furniture, too, reflected in the floor. Nancy walked barefoot across the floor. The air smelled of beeswax and, in light whiffs, naphthalene.

She went to her bedroom, where on the wall-to-wall carpet lay her open valise and, by it, department-store bags with the clothes she'd bought still in them. She stretched out on her unmade bed, the white satin spread thrown down to the foot. It seemed to her she heard a dull thump somewhere in the apartment, and she went rigid, listening. It didn't reoccur, but the silence seemed to have its own sound, and, rigid still, she listened to this. Slowly, she got up and put on the dressing gown taken from the back of a chair, and, with a faint tingling throughout her, she went out into the hallway to look into her mother and father's bedroom, to make sure there was no one but herself in the apartment. Back in her room, she sat on the edge of her bed for a while, motionless.

On her bedside table was a white telephone. She wanted to call someone, but about everyone she thought of calling, she thought, no, not him. She called her mother in Amagansett.

In her low voice, her mother said, "You'll be careful, please, driving back to Boston."

"I'll drive carefully, but very fast."

Her mother said, "Yes," and sighed a little.

Nancy wandered again around the apartment, looking for someone who was not, she knew, there. She was always looking for what was not there.

Back in the living room, she examined, on the mantelpiece of the fireplace, two ice pails that had been on the mantelpiece for as long as she could remember. They were Berlin porcelain, brought from Berlin by her mother's parents when they came to New York as refugees, and for a moment she wondered if for them these reminders of life in Berlin still hurt. At the sides of the buckets were golden lions' heads biting on golden rings; on their fronts were perspective views, one of a country road and trees with tiny people seen from the back wearing black and red clothes, and the other of a palace and a square before it with tiny figures in red and black, also seen from the back. Nancy's parents didn't talk about Berlin, or maybe she did not want to hear about Berlin. Or, maybe, her parents didn't want her to know.

She was, she told herself, a spoiled girl who did everything she could to be light-spirited, if not superficial. And though her parents would have denied this, she felt they encouraged her to be spoiled and light-spirited, even, she accused herself, superficial. They may have sighed at her behavior, but they seemed pleased by her daring, for they had bought her a sleek sports car.

If she wanted a different life from the life they could offer her, they supported her in wanting that different life. They worried if she went into one of her dark moods and stayed closed up in her room, as if she did this because of them. She tried to reassure them that her dark moods had nothing to do with them, who were too indulgent of her, their only child, and for their sakes she was light-spirited, even, yes, superficial; but they still felt they were at fault for her moods. She herself had no idea where these moods came from, any more than she knew what she was always looking for.

She had a long weekend before leaving for Boston, and felt restless, without knowing just what she was restless about.

She wanted to call someone, but about everyone she thought of calling, she decided, no, not him. She yawned and stretched out her arms. I know the person I want to call, she thought; I want to call Vinnie Tasso. He was her former colleague from a summer internship in a publishing house.

He said he didn't feel like going out.

"Oh, come on, Vinnie."

"Oh, come on, Vinnie. Oh, come on, Vinnie. Oh, come on, Vinnie." He whined. "Everyone is always telling me, oh, come on, Vinnie."

"Come on, Vinnie."

"All right, all right."

She went to him just after dark.

Vinnie lived in a small apartment in Chelsea with a view of a ginkgo tree in the streetlight. He did layout for a glossy magazine; a brick wall was covered with overlapping layout sheets and photographs with blocks of text and lines drawn zigzagging across them, and an electric fan, turning from side to side, made the sheets flutter. Vinnie was thin and short and sexless, even in his own view of himself, but he didn't seem to mind this. He was, he himself said, more social than sexual.

He opened a bottle of sparkling white wine and, handing Nancy a glass, asked her what she'd done in Amagansett over the summer. She said he wouldn't be interested, and he said she was right, he wouldn't be.

"Then let's not sit here," Nancy said. "Let's finish the wine and go to your bar."

"Why is it that you need me to take you to the bar?"

"So you can introduce me to your friends."

"You've already met everyone I know there who could possibly be of any interest to you, and they weren't of any interest."

"You didn't make any new friends over the summer?"

"I made a lot a friends, but none of them would interest you."

"Why don't you leave that to me?"

The bar, in the West Village, had a dance floor in strobe lights where young men and women danced together or alone, and around the dance floor were cloth-covered tables, waiters in black vests.

Nancy danced with Vinnie, who said she was a bad dancer. He was right, but she was equal to anyone around her in the pleasure she took from the place. Swaying her hips, she raised her hands high and snapped her fingers and laughed. She was tall, and had long, loose, light russet hair and pale brown eyes, and her almost matte white skin was freckled across her delicate, bony chin and cheeks. She was wearing a long, full red dress with tiny embossed medallions sewn along the bodice, and on her long, narrow feet red espadrilles laced up, criss-cross, above her ankles.

Back at their table with Vinnie, she looked at the dancers in the strobe light that made them disappear and appear, disappear and appear, lit in different positions.

Nancy asked, "Who's that?"

"Who?"

"There, standing at the bar, wearing chinos and a Columbia University sweatshirt."

The guy standing at the bar had very short black hair, and his black beard shadowed the taut white skin of his angular face. The wide collar of his sweatshirt revealed his muscular neck, which appeared, in itself, to expose all his muscular body. Black chest hair curled above the ribbed collar. The corners of his mouth curved in a slight, fixed smile; he looked around at everyone and at no one with large black eyes.

"That's Aaron," Vinnie said.

"Aaron?"

"Aaron Cohen."

"Let me guess. He's Jewish," Nancy said.

Vinnie said, "You're really good at picking up on names."

When, again, she looked at the guy at the bar, he turned his back toward her. He leaned on the bar, and his broad shoulder blades stretched the cloth of the sweatshirt.

Vinnie said, "He's not just Jewish; he comes from a really strict Hasidic family in the Bronx."

"That guy, standing there, comes from a Hasidic family?"

Vinnie, who liked to think he knew everything about everyone, said he knew everything about Aaron: he was brought up to let his forelocks grow in long curls, to wear a black overcoat, a black skull cap and a black fedora, and black trousers with a very low crotch, and all those shawls and strings tied around him under his black jacket—the whole bit.

"Really?"

"Yes, really and truly. He used to have to do things I'll bet you've never even heard of."

"Like what?"

"You ask me? Everybody knows what a Catholic has to do. A Catholic has to practice sexual abstinence, that's what a Catholic has to do. I don't know what Aaron had to do. Anyway, he gave it all up."

"Why?"

"I don't know."

"Why does he come here?"

"I think he comes here because it's as far from Hasidic Jews as he can get."

"Does he ever pick up a girl?"

"I've only ever seen him go off on his own."

"Does he at least talk with anyone?"

"What he does is he stands at the bar and drinks beer and looks around, and if he thinks anyone is looking at him he looks away."

Aaron Cohen's shoulder blades moved under his sweatshirt whenever he raised his bottle of beer or lowered it.

Vinnie slouched in his bentwood chair while searching the bar, it seemed, for someone else, anyone but Aaron Cohen.

"You don't want me to meet him," Nancy said.

Half smiling, Vinnie said, "I'd like to know what you expect from him."

"For Christ's sake, what do you think I expect from him?"

"I don't know, but why do you want to meet him unless you expect something from him?"

"Come on, go talk with him and bring him back."

"Aaron doesn't talk much."

"How do you know him, if he doesn't talk?"

"He talks with me because I talk with him, the way I talk with everybody."

"Come on, I'd like to meet him."

Vinnie slouched back on his chair and only after a while lurched forward and said, "Oh all right," and got up, his long, thin neck, torso, and legs swaying. He went to the bar to order drinks from the bartender and, as if incidentally, started to talk with Aaron, whose head turned sideways, so the light from behind the bar showed up his neck. When Nancy saw Vinnie nod toward her, she knew he was asking Aaron to come to their table. Aaron stood back from the bar to look in her direction, and she quickly glanced over her shoulder to see if there was anybody behind her. But there was no one. The table behind her was empty. She turned back to Aaron, who was walking toward the table with Vinnie.

He had clear features, and though his beard showed he appeared to have just shaved because his skin was slightly glossy. As Vinnie introduced him to Nancy, he smiled more, but he didn't seem to know what to do until Vinnie said, "Sit," and he drew the sleeves of his sweatshirt further up his forearms before he sat, then he smiled at Nancy and said, in a low voice, "Hi," and she said, "Hi," and she smiled, too. Nancy liked his smile.

Vinnie helped her, as he always did. He sat between her and Aaron and said to Aaron, "Don't ask Nancy to dance. She's a terrible dancer."

"I don't know how to dance," Aaron said.

Standing, Vinnie said, "Then you both have a lot to say to each other, so I'm going to make the rounds."

"Stay with us, Vinnie," Aaron said.

Tapping him on the head, Vinnie said, "You still think it's wrong to sit with a woman, do you?" He picked up his drink and left.

The strange sense occurred to Nancy of someone standing behind her, about to grab her; the sense was strange and
at the same time familiar: she felt that someone, or something, was always there behind her and about to grab her,
and when it occurred it startled her. Pulling away, she hit
her hip against the edge of the round table and her cocktail
splashed in its glass.

"Are you all right?" Aaron asked.

Laughing a loud laugh, Nancy thought how sometimes
she could almost be vulgar when she was loud. She pressed
a hand to the base of her throat to repress her loudness.
"I'm all right." But she was still startled.

Aaron's shoulders sank a little as he resigned himself to
staying with her until she said he could go, or so Nancy
thought. If he was a Hasid, she didn't know what he felt
about a woman sitting next to him in a bar. But what he
felt was up to him, not her, because he had his reasons for
coming to the bar and he could have made some excuse and
got up and left her if he wanted to. Still, it was strange that
he was a good-looking Hasid in a sweatshirt drinking beer
from a bottle while she sipped at her Manhattan.

"Where do you live?" Nancy asked him.

"On the Upper West Side. And you, where do you live?"

"On the Upper East Side."

Aaron nodded.

Well, they'd got that far, but Nancy didn't know how to
go further, so they both looked at the dancers in the strobe
light.

She asked, "Is it true that you don't know how to dance?"

"I've never tried."

This offered her a chance, but she felt too disoriented to take it. She said, "Well, Vinnie is right, I'm a terrible dancer. You wouldn't learn anything from me."

"Anyway," he said, "I'm not really interested in learning to dance."

"Then I could ask you what you are interested in."

Now he laughed, and she knew he wouldn't say, and she asked herself if she was really interested in him. No, not really. He was too strange, at least for her. She'd never met an ex-Hasid before; she wondered if she'd ever met a Hasid, however often she'd seen them walking up and down West Forty-Seventh Street. In their business, they were supposed to carry in their heavy overcoats millions of dollars' worth of diamonds and gold, or so she'd heard. But she couldn't see Aaron in that way. She couldn't see him in any way. And she thought she'd like to leave.

She said, "I guess I'd better go," and she stood and he, too, stood, which she thought was polite of him, and as she walked to the exit he followed, which was even more polite. Instead of stopping at the door to say goodbye, Aaron opened the door and waited for her to go out onto the sidewalk, and he went out with her. She could have said goodbye to him then, but, disoriented, she walked on, and because he followed her she stopped and waited for him to stop beside her. She asked herself, What's going on? He was looking out at the traffic in the street, as if he were alone. And there came to Nancy the feeling that she, too, was alone, that if there was anything between them, it was that they were both alone against whatever it was that pulled them both from behind. She asked, "What about walking together for a while?" and he turned to her the smile she had liked and he said, "I'd like that."

There was tenderness in Aaron's angular face, and he looked at her as if he were waiting for her to decide which direction they'd take. She noticed that his black eyebrows almost met over his nose.

Nancy shook her long hair and said, "I like New York when it's hot."

They walked by people sitting on the steep steps to high stoops and the open front doors of narrow brick town houses, the street filled with shadows cast by streetlights through the trees. Though the air was still, the sultry stillness seemed within itself to be restless and about to break out in wild, dance-like movements. A greater sense of restlessness was about to break out into wild movement in the traffic and pedestrians along wide Fourteenth Street, where stores opened onto the sidewalk. They crossed Fourteenth Street to walk up Eighth Avenue, where the cars and the people were congested as if for a carnival, or for a carnival that everyone had come for but that hadn't yet begun, the dancing already promised in the honking of car horns and people yelling. Nancy and Aaron walked past a man playing a saxophone and a woman tap-dancing on a sheet of plywood.

When they were passing the Port Authority building, Aaron asked Nancy if she was tired and would like him to hail a taxi.

"I'd like to go on walking," she said. "And you?"

He raised a shoulder and let it drop, then said, "I like walking," and Nancy smiled a little at what she thought was the Jewishness of his gesture and his intonation.

She didn't mind what direction they took, a direction
that, it seemed to her, was taken for them by New York.

They crossed Forty-Second Street, and went on up
Eighth Avenue to Columbus Circle, walking over gratings
from which hot and fetid air blew up, sometimes with tiny
birds' feathers, and in the shafts below the gratings were
dark spaces that were lit by the burning, dim bare bulbs
down there. The sidewalks were packed with people, the
avenue jammed with traffic, and it seemed that the restlessness in the hot night would be, if it did break out into
movement, violent, and there was an exciting expectation
even in this. Nancy wanted something to happen, and she
felt that New York on a hot night would make it happen.

A police car, its siren wailing, raced round Columbus Circle.

On the other side of Columbus Circle, Central Park West
was almost empty of pedestrians and traffic. On one side of
the avenue were the illuminated lobbies of the apartment
houses seen through open doors, the doormen standing just
outside for the coolness that came from the park across the
avenue, beyond the blackened granite wall, where lights
shone here and there among the dark trees.

Nancy thought that surely Aaron must be wondering if
she was going to walk all the way with him, wherever all
the way was, but, again, she let herself drift along.

They stopped on a corner for the light to change, and
Nancy became aware of him standing beside her, of his
body beneath his sweatshirt and chinos. Aaron didn't move
even when the light changed, and Nancy, to get him moving, nudged him a little with her hip.

In the middle of the street, he asked, "Are you sure you don't want a taxi now?"

He had a deliberate way of talking, as if studied, and, as studied as it was, she wondered if he meant he wanted her to leave him.

"Well, I'm not going to walk through the park at night," she said.

He said, "I wouldn't let you," and she followed him as they crossed the street to the next block. Not knowing what he wanted, not having known all the time they'd walked together, she followed him when he turned at Eighty-Ninth Street, and she went with him and they crossed Columbus Avenue to continue down Eighty-Ninth Street, and when he stopped in front of a brownstone, where he said he lived, she stopped with him. All the restlessness of the late summer night seemed to be her restlessness, not his.

As if she hadn't quite understood, she asked, "So this is where you live?"

He repeated, "This is where I live."

She heard herself ask, as if she were at a distance from her speaking self, "Do you want me to come in?"

Blinking, he smiled, but now not the smile she liked: a smile of only the corners of his lips that she read as, he was sorry, but all he had wanted was the walk, and it was time to say goodnight.

What had he been thinking on their walk? Whatever he'd been thinking she didn't want to know. Once again, she had a sense that he was alone, and she felt alone with him, as if each being alone was what had kept them walking together.

She thought: You could read anything you wanted into someone's silence.

Yet she said, "I'd understand if you don't want me to come up."

"No, no," he said, but she could tell he didn't want her to.

"Then, with all the walking we've done, I wouldn't mind sitting down for ten minutes."

"Oh sure," Aaron said, but he didn't move.

"So," Nancy asked, "I mean, if you don't want me to come up, I'll sit for ten minutes on the step here. Maybe you feel it's wrong to be alone with a woman, especially in an apartment."

"I don't have an apartment, just a room."

"Is that what you don't want me to see, that you live in just one room?"

"I'm not ashamed of living in one room."

"But you are about having a woman in it with you."

"Sometimes women have come up to visit me."

"Alone?"

He blinked rapidly and his tight smile had gone. "Sometimes alone."

"Then there has to be something in your room you don't want me to see."

He said, "There's nothing in my room I wouldn't want anyone in the world to see."

And he touched Nancy's elbow to lead her up the steep cement steps to the stoop. His movements as he took his keys from the hip pocket of his chinos became easy; his entire way of moving suddenly became easy. He swung open the wide front door, with three small Gothic windows in it, for Nancy to go in first.

In the entranceway, lit by a dim overhead globe, she said, "This house is so quiet."

Aaron said, "It's always quiet."

He didn't seem to know if he should lead the way up the stairs or let her go first and follow her, and Nancy took it on herself to go up the wooden stairs, dark brown and varnished, with wooden spheres on the newel posts. The stairs creaked. She stopped on a landing and let him go ahead of her to his room, which was two more flights up, at the back.

He unlocked the door, then held out his hand for Nancy to go in first.

The small room had wainscoting, in Gothic arches, all around the walls. A lot of the furniture, too, was Gothic—a long, refectory-like table, a chair with a Gothic back, a bookcase that was a tall, narrow Gothic arch. The bed, covered by an old khaki army blanket, was pushed against a small fireplace, and above the mantel of the fireplace hung a crucifix. Nancy stopped short before it. The body was matte white, the face of Christ raised and staring up in agony, and the cross was black. Aaron passed in front of Nancy to open a window.

He said, "It's hot in here, and, I'm sorry, there's a closed-in smell of not very clean laundry."

Nancy turned away from the crucifix to face Aaron, who would not in her presence even look at the figure of Christ crucified, as if he knew she would embarrass herself by asking him why he, a Jew, an Orthodox Jew, had a crucifix hanging in his room; but it was just this question that she wanted to ask, but didn't because she didn't want to embarrass him, so there they were, two Jews, not able to speak about a presence that now appeared to hang over them in the room.

"Would you like some cold tea?" Aaron asked her.

"That would be nice," she answered quietly.

He left her to go behind a screen to his small kitchen. She sat at the foot of the military-like bed. The table was covered with books, some lying open, and papers. Aaron came toward her with two tall glasses of tea, ice cubes clinking.

"You're studying," she said.

"I've been studying all summer."

"What?"

"Oh," he said, and once again shrugged.

Nancy put her glass on the floor and, weary, asked, "I need to lie down. Can I lie on your bed?"

"I'll need to change the pillow case," Aaron said.

"It'll be all right." She put the glass of tea, hardly drunk, on a corner of the table; she untied the laces and kicked off her espadrilles and lay back on Aaron's bed, her head on his pillow. She closed her eyes, then opened them and saw Aaron, sitting on the wooden chair, watching her. She asked, "Will you lie beside me? Just lie beside me, that's all."

He took off his shoes and came to the bed. Putting one knee on the edge, he swiveled his body round and lay flat beside her, his arms alongside his body, his head at the edge of the pillow. He swallowed a lot, which made his neck convulse. Though he closed his eyes, she knew from his swallowing and convulsing neck that he didn't fall asleep. When she touched his shoulder, he opened his eyes, but didn't look at her.

"I am embarrassing you," she said.

"A little," he said.

Then she closed her eyes and, wondering where she was and what she was doing there, she fell asleep. She woke to find him asleep beside her, his body turned towards her, his arms tightly folded about his chest, his knees bent, his face half pressed into the pillow. The yellowish ceiling light was still on, but the gray-blue dawn light through the window was stronger. Quietly, so as not to disturb him, Nancy got up, slipped on her espadrilles and tied the laces, then went out and closed the door behind her.

Outside, she found the dawn sky reddish and reflected in the windshields of the cars parked along the empty street.

The doorman who had the night shift came out and opened the taxi door for her. In the apartment, she looked around the rooms.

In the bathroom off her bedroom she showered and brushed her teeth. Wrapped in a large towel, another towel around her head, she again looked around the apartment. Nothing in it, not one thing, would have indicated to someone who didn't know that the people who lived there were Jewish.

She slept, and in the afternoon called Vinnie to ask for Aaron's telephone number.

"I don't think you should get involved with Aaron. He'll be leaving New York soon."

"How do you know?"

"I know everything."

"Where will he be going?"

"Listen," Vinnie said, "don't get involved. You have nothing in common with him, nothing at all. Forget about him."

"Okay," she said.

"I'm telling you again, forget about him."

"Okay, okay."

Vinnie invited her to a party that night. She didn't want to go, but she said she would. It was Saturday, and she always wanted to go out on a Saturday.

Sunday morning, her parents returned from Amagansett. Her mother said that Nancy was right, the Hamptons got lonely with all the people gone; and anyway it was time to get back to the city, where Nancy's father had been coming to work during the week.

She had brunch with her parents in a small restaurant on an East Side cross street, and afterward she said she'd do some shopping. The sky was low and gray, the lowness and grayness seeming to reach down to the ground, and the air was suddenly chill. She didn't go shopping when she left her parents, but walked over to Central Park. In the chill she drew the silk scarf from about her neck, covered her head with it, and tied the corners under her chin, and she walked slowly, as if she weren't going anyplace but had come into the park just to stroll. She left by the Eighty-Second Street exit and went up to Eighty-Ninth Street and west on it to the house with steep cement steps leading to a high stoop and the wide wooden door with the three Gothic windows, where Aaron lived. She examined the names, each with a black button by it, at the side of the door. Only one space was blank. She pressed the bell and as she did she leaned toward the door to listen for the sound of a bell ringing from deep inside, but she heard nothing. As no one came to the door, she turned away. On the sidewalk, she looked up once more at the wooden front door of the house. Then the door opened and Aaron Cohen, in brown corduroy trousers and a dark brown cardigan, stepped out onto the stoop.

She called up, "You're here?"

"I guess I am," he answered.

"Vinnie told me not to bother you."

"Vinnie is filled with advice he gives to other people but never gives to himself."

"That's Vinnie."

Under the cardigan, Aaron wore a white shirt, the collar open, and around his neck was a thin gold chain, and Nancy wondered if some religious medal was dangling from that chain.

"Should I come up?" she asked.

Aaron laughed and said, "I wouldn't know how to stop you if I didn't want you to come up."

Nancy asked, "Should I think I'm forcing myself on you?"

"Think of it this way," Aaron said, "not that you're forcing yourself on me but that I always have to leave it to other people to make the first move."

"All right. I'm making the first move."

Aaron let her go ahead into the entry hall, where she untied the knot of her silk scarf under her chin and, pulling at a corner, slid it and draped it about her neck, a gesture she connected with an older woman.

She said, "This house really is so dark and quiet."

They climbed the stairs side by side, Nancy running her hand along the highly varnished handrail and then over the spheres on the newel posts. Sometimes she and Aaron bumped lightly into one another.

The door to his room was open, and light shone from

inside. She went in first and, as though trying to check everything against her memory of it, looked around slowly.

The crucifix, the white, tortured Christ nailed to a black cross, was hanging over the fireplace.

Nancy unbuckled the belt of her trench coat, unbuttoned it, and held it out to Aaron, but when she realized she was presuming on his politeness she took it back and said, "I'm sorry. Tell me where to put my coat."

"Give it to me," he said, "and I'll hang it in my closet."

She went to his work table but, standing over it, she stopped herself from looking at the books and papers.

She said to Aaron, "Here I am, about to look at what you're writing."

"You can look at whatever you want."

"And supposing I come across some secret of yours among your papers?"

"That'd be fine with me."

"You don't have secrets?"

"I don't."

Nancy sat on the Gothic chair and Aaron in an old armchair under a floor lamp where she supposed he read, one of his books on the floor. The light made each short strand of his thick, black hair shine.

Looking at him, Nancy thought, Give in, let go and give in—but she had no idea what she would be letting go of to give in to.

She asked, "Do you ever have moods?"

"Moods?"

"Moods, when you feel, oh, that all you want is to lie in the dark, just lie there?"

Aaron lowered his eyes, and she thought that she was making herself vulnerable to him by talking about moods, but she couldn't help talking; it was as if she was talking against his silence, trying to get him to agree that they shared some mood.

She said, "I tell myself, when I'm in one of those moods, that I must not give in, that I must never give in, that I must go out and see people, people as superficial as I am, because I never know what might be in the dark."

His eyes still lowered, Aaron appeared to be thinking of how he would answer her, but when he looked at her his expression was that he wouldn't be able to explain, and his inability to explain made his look one of pain.

All at once impatient with his evasiveness, impatient with him for presuming she wouldn't understand what he understood, Nancy rose from the chair and stood facing him, and he stood because she did; as a reproach, her voice high, she asked, "Don't you ever have longings?" and as soon as she had spoken it seemed to her that she heard her own words, heard them as Aaron heard them, and they had the meaning Aaron heard in them, the meaning that suddenly coursed through her as a sensation in her body, and she became still.

He quietly turned away and went to the window. He said, "It's raining."

She said in a very quiet voice, "Are you leaving New York, like Vinnie said?"

"Vinnie's right for once. I am."

"Where will you go after you leave New York?"

"I'll be going to a monastery in upstate New York for final instruction before my baptism."

Nancy's voice had an edge of accusation. "Your baptism?"

"To become a Catholic."

"You, a Hasid, becoming a Catholic?"

"Who told you that?"

"Vinnie told me."

"Vinnie exaggerates, you can't believe anything Vinnie says about anyone."

Nancy tried to laugh, but the laugh came out a cackle. "So you're not a Hasid?"

"I'll always be what I am, a Jew."

"Then, isn't it enough for you, being a Jew?"

His voice flat, he said, "I have mine, you have your own longings."

Her voice sharpened as though accusing him of longings that had to be false when she said, "Yes, I have my own longings, yes, I do. And they're the longings of a Jew, because that's what I am, too, a Jew." But she had no idea what the longings of a Jew could be.

He turned again to the window, against which the rain ran in rivulets, and Nancy, as if his turning away made all her high feelings fall away, went to stand beside him and to look through the distorting rivulets out to the street below.

Her voice fell low when she said, contrite, "I wouldn't be able to guess what a Catholic longs for, just that it must be strange, and it makes me feel that you must be strange."

"I'm not strange," he said.

"You are to me."

"But you don't know me."

"I don't, and I suppose I won't. What will you do when you're a Catholic?"

"The monastery runs a farm, so I'll be taking care of pigs and sheep and cows while I'm there."

As if she didn't hear, staring ahead, Nancy went to sit on the Gothic chair. She felt tears collect on her lower lids, and she raised her fingers to wipe them away, but the more she wiped them away the more they collected, until they coursed down her cheeks and fingers. She remained on the chair, her shoulders hunched and her knees pressed together.

When Aaron came to her with a box of tissues, she drew a number out, and said, "Thank you," and wiped her eyes and blew her nose.

"I'm sorry," she said.

"I am too," he said.

"Don't think you did anything to hurt me," she said quietly. "You didn't. I know you'd never hurt anyone."

"But you are hurt," he said.

Her fingertips raised again to both her eyes, the tears streamed down her hands to her wrists.

She said, "I don't know why I'm crying." And after a moment she laughed and stood.

The gold chain was tight about Aaron's neck, which appeared to be slightly damp. Whatever was hanging on the chain was hidden beneath his shirt, in the hair of his chest. She touched his chest.

"You would never give in just to having some fun."

He smiled.

She wiped her eyes and blew her nose again.

"Maybe I should go," she said.

"Maybe," he said.

She stared at the balled-up wet tissue in her open hand,

then looked around the room, as if what she should do with that wet tissue were her first concern. She closed it in a fist.

"Is it still raining?" she asked.

"I think it's stopping."

"Tell me, why do you go to that bar?"

Now, unexpectedly, a lively spirit came into his voice, and a lively spirit came into his body, too, because he rocked his shoulders in a way he hadn't before, as if he had repressed the spirit but now let it out, daring himself because he knew she was leaving, and he said, "To find out if I'm tempted."

"Tempted by what?"

And here, with a great suddenness, he smiled such a wide smile, his teeth strong and bright, that his whole self appeared exposed, a self made stronger and brighter by his asking, "Don't you know?"

"I don't."

And he said, "By you," and his smile was beautiful.

He was to become a monk, and monks were not meant to be seductive. Not knowing how to respond, and thinking, Why am I so silly? Nancy asked, "Will you get my coat for me, please?"

He went to his closet, unhooked a hanger, and slipped her trench coat from it, then returned to her, holding it open. She turned and inserted her arms into the sleeves and put the wad of wet tissue into a pocket.

"My scarf?" she asked.

"It's around your shoulders."

She raised the triangle from her shoulders and covered her head with it and tied the ends of the corners in a knot under her chin. She did this slowly, slowly buttoned her trench coat, and buckled her belt. She thought of herself as a woman in control.

"Well, then," Nancy said, "I don't suppose there's any reason for us to see one another again," and she held out her hand.

He took it, but he said, "Maybe not."

She was the first to withdraw her hand from his. "Don't come downstairs with me," she said. "I can go on my own."

He went ahead of her to open the door to his room.

"Well then," she said, "bye."

"Bye."

She couldn't help herself. She reached out and, leaning towards him, put her arms around him. It took him a moment to raise his arms to hold her as she held him. She pressed her face against the side of his face.

He kissed her on a cheek, then for a moment held her more closely to him before he let his arms drop, and she knew she must let him go and stand back and turn away. When she reached the top of the stairs on the landing she heard the door to his room close. Halfway down the flight of stairs, she stopped and sat on a step for a moment.

Leaves fallen in the gutters were wet, and the leaves on the trees were dripping.

As she walked, she sensed that music she had never heard before was going round her mind and she couldn't hum it.

Nancy spent Sunday evening in with her parents, which surprised them. Because she was thinking about Aaron, it occurred to her at dinner that he would have been a very strange presence at the table with her parents, and because she couldn't see him there, she said, as if urged to confront her parents with someone she doubted very much they would have known, "Vinnie introduced me to a Hasid."

Her mother asked, "How is Vinnie? He makes me laugh."

"He tries," Nancy said. "He sends his best."

Surprised, her father asked, "Where did you meet a Hasid?"

"In a bar in the Village."

"You met a Hasid in a bar in the Village? Seems unlikely to me."

"Well, Vinnie said he's Hasid."

Nancy's mother said, "Maybe he was joking."

"He's becoming a Catholic," Nancy said.

Her mother, who never quite concentrated on what was being said, asked, "Vinnie is becoming a Catholic?"

And Nancy's father, who always tried to counter the vagueness of his wife by stating the facts, as if the facts were a little judgment against her, said, "Vinnie is a Catholic."

"I wasn't talking about Vinnie," Nancy said. "I said that I met a Hasid who's becoming a Catholic."

"Where on earth did you meet a Hasid?' her mother asked.

"As I said, in a bar, in Greenwich Village."

"How could you have met him in a bar in Greenwich Village?" her mother asked.

"You have vague ideas about Greenwich Village," Nancy's father told his wife.

Nancy knew that her parents loved each other, but she did think her father sometimes taunted her mother.

Her father said to her, "If the person you met is a Hasid converting to being a Catholic, he would be a very lonely man. His family would sit shiva for him, and he'd die to them."

"I think Aaron is lonely," Nancy said. "Yes, he is."

"Aaron?" her mother asked.

"The Hasid I met."

"I'm sorry for him," her mother said. "Do you know him well enough to invite him to a meal?"

"I don't think he'd come."

"Does he imagine we'd object to him?"

"No, no, not that. He'd just feel that somehow he doesn't belong. In fact, I think he never feels, or has ever felt, that he belongs."

"What else do you know about him?" her father asked.

"Not much. He was wearing a Columbia University sweatshirt, so maybe he was a student there."

"That would mean he'd already come a long way from being a Hasid."

"I've heard," Nancy's mother said, "that the clothes they wear are from the eighteenth century."

"Yes, I've heard," Nancy repeated, and she thought, as she had thought before: there was nothing in the family apartment that she could have identified as Jewish, not a mezuzah on the jamb of the door to the apartment. She didn't believe that her parents had done this intentionally, but that it happened, nor did she know what had happened to her parents before they came to New York—what had happened to them in Berlin, what had happened to their families in Germany. She knew this: that when her father learned that he would be banned from university, he quickly went home and with her mother packed two suitcases and locked the door and they went to the train station and boarded the next train to Amsterdam.

But Nancy did not know how her parents had arrived in New York or how the Biedermeier furniture and the Berlin ice buckets had followed them, and she did not know why she held back from asking.

After dinner, her mother asked her if she was going out, and, again, she said no, and she joined them for coffee in what was called the office, where her father sat at his desk in a leather chair. On his desk were international magazines on wine, and on bookshelves, books in English and French and German and Russian (her father was born in Russia but moved to Berlin with his parents when he was a boy); and there were books on viticulture and vineyards, some of them large, bulky presentation copies. Nancy knew this much: that after her parents arrived in New York, her father was hired by a refugee family who had reestablished in New York their old family wine business from Germany, and as the family died out her father, as though a surviving member, became the head. But the business was now running down and Nancy's father thought of selling, but didn't. Her mother sat in a small, upholstered armchair in front of the desk. She was born in Berlin.

And because of Aaron, because of the continuing loneliness that she felt isolated him as a Jew, a loneliness that maybe was also hers because she, too, was a Jew, she wanted to know more from her parents about what had happened to them before New York, what had happened to them as Jews among Jews, but she didn't know how to engage them.

She asked, suggesting that the thought came to her incidentally, "Don't I remember you once trying to search for some relatives?"

"We're still trying," her father said.

Her mother abruptly said, "Nan, darling, ask Vinnie to come to dinner with us while you're away. He does make us both laugh."

She took the cup of coffee Nancy held out to her and said, "Thank you," and Nancy thought, too, that her parents' rather formal after-dinner coffee in her father's office was from a past Nancy knew little about.

Then it occurred to Nancy that there was something so obvious in all that her parents didn't tell her about their Jewish pasts that she wanted to expose it, and she said curtly, "Well, thank you both for what you won't tell me."

Her father picked up a letter opener and held it between both hands, and said, "We really don't know."

Nancy said, "I don't want any coffee. I think I'll go lie on my bed and read. I have a lot of reading to do for my courses."

"Oh, don't go, Nan," her mother said.

She knew that she had hurt her parents, and she was sorry, for how could she blame them for not telling her what they themselves couldn't know? Her mother said, "Tell us what you've been reading," and this made Nancy feel they were trying to make up for having hurt her, though she had hurt them.

No, Nancy thought, her parents weren't interested in hearing about her reading, not now, and she herself was not interested in telling them; but she and her parents were in that strange mode when nothing that was said was meant, and there was no way of knowing what was meant, not, certainly, when Nancy said that she had noted something in Henry James's novel *The Golden Bowl* that she wondered about and if it had been noted by anyone else. As she spoke she thought, what possible relevance could there be between Henry James and the past history of her parents, who didn't know about their lost relatives and their lost friends?

Her father said, "Your mother is tired."

"No, no, I'm not. Tell us, Nan darling, tell us, we want to know."

In her mother's vagueness there was a deep, stunned calm, and in the deep calm a sense of always trying to understand all that was beyond understanding, and so the apparent lack of focus in her eyes.

"It doesn't matter," Nancy said.

"Please," her mother said.

They were, Nancy thought, all of them, being stilted.

"Here it is. In the novel, the Roman prince, about to marry in London, expects his relatives to arrive from Italy for the wedding, and among them is his younger brother, whose wife, 'of the Hebrew race, with a portion that had gilded the pill, was not in a condition to travel.' And this is the only reference to a Jew in the book."

Maybe her parents didn't comment because they wondered why their daughter made such a point of the reference in Henry James, but Nancy persisted. "I keep asking myself what he meant by 'with a portion that gilded the pill'?" She thought, here she was trying to find anti-Semitism in Henry James to get her parents talking, and she knew that she was, with a righteousness that had to do with an inner opposition to Aaron, stressing the text, looking for a subtext that was probably not there. But as they drank their coffee, Nancy sensed there was some subtext in her parents' silence, and if it was not about their being Jewish, she could not imagine what it could be about.

There was still something not said, all of them waiting for what was not said to be heard, maybe to be said by someone who was not in fact present, and yet somehow present.

Her mother appeared to go into a reverie, and, leaning her head to the side and looking away, she said quietly, "Die Luft ist kühl und es dunkelt, und ruhig fließt der Rhein."

Her father said, "The air is cool and darkens, and the Rhine flows calmly on."

Nancy asked, "Heine?"

And her father said, "Yes, Heine."

And her mother smiled at her for recognizing the name of the poet who wrote that beautiful line.

Nancy kissed them both and said good night, and left them to go to her room, where she lay on her bed in the dark, until she told herself not to, and she switched on a light to read.

Early the next morning, she breakfasted with her parents, who had come from their bed to be with her before she left for Boston, and she felt more lonely than she had ever felt on her way from them.

She had a student apartment on Beacon Hill. The house, like many of the houses on Beacon Hill, was brick, with a black door and a brass knocker, but where she lived the old Yankee families didn't live any longer; the house was on the somewhat dilapidated side of the hill, the door scuffed and the brass knocker askew.

The apartment had a bedroom in the front and a kitchen at the back, with a striped Indian blanket nailed to the architrave of the doorless doorway between the two, and beyond the kitchen was the bathroom. As soon as she dropped her suitcase on the floor at the end of her bed, she sat on the edge and telephoned Manos, who was supposed to be expecting her. The bed faced a small fireplace, and while the telephone at the other end of the line was ringing she looked at the BU white ceramic beer stein, the incense sticks in a hand-thrown vase, the branch of maple leaves that had been on the mantelpiece when she'd left two months before. Manos answered and said he'd been waiting for her to telephone. There was a student party that night they could go to.

She said, "I was hoping to see you on your own."

She didn't understand why he didn't want to see her on his own, or maybe she did understand, or would if she figured it out. She was feeling too light-headed to think about it.

Darkness had fallen by the time Manos arrived and found her, barefoot and in jeans and a sweatshirt, reading a scholarly book on the novel that she should have read over the summer. She really, really didn't want to go out, she said, but she made herself get up and change and go out with him. He was a big man, with small hands and feet and dark circles around his darker eyes. He was a premedical student. At the party, he talked for so long with the friend who was giving it, also premed, that Nancy wandered off on her own, as she guessed he wanted her to.

She made the tour, a drink in a raised hand, looking for someone who had a story to tell her. Not finding one, she returned to Manos and said she really, really wanted to go home, and he said, sure, he'd drive her. In his car he rested his hand on her thigh as he drove, and she wondered if this meant he wanted to spend the night with her. But in the street he didn't park his car, didn't even shut off the engine, so she knew he wasn't going to come in with her.

He said, "Nancy, things have changed."

She reached out and put her arms around him and kissed his forehead and said, "Sure," and felt an odd sense of relief. She stumbled on the way to the door. He waited until she had opened it and closed it behind her before he drove off.

For two weeks, she devoted herself to her studies, especially the work of Henry James. She didn't go to any parties, and when Manos telephoned her, which he did often, she said she felt they shouldn't see one another for a while.

Four weeks into the semester she decided to go to New York for the weekend to be with her parents. She missed them, she missed New York. She cut one class and left Friday afternoon, and on the way noted that the leaves of the birch trees along the highways had turned autumn yellow.

Her parents were both in their sixties. Nancy had been a latecomer in their marriage. At dinner, she told them what she'd been doing at BU but not what she planned to do with a master's degree in English when she got it. When her father asked, "How's Manos getting on with his medical studies?" Nancy said, "I'm not dating Manos anymore," and her father, with a severe frown, asked, "Why?" Nancy shrugged. Again, her father asked, "Why?" but her mother, looking steadily at him, stopped him from asking more about Nancy's love life. He said, "Funny the way Greeks are always studying to be doctors or lawyers."

Early snow fell lightly, and Nancy went out on Sunday afternoon to walk in the falling flakes. She found herself walking across Central Park, where the snow was settling on the withered leaves still on the trees. Flakes hit her face as she stood in front of the house where Aaron had lived, and where he might still live, or where someone might know about him. But as she, blinking, looked up the snow-covered stairs and stoop, on which there were no footsteps, it came to her as a matter of fact that while she had been away she had exaggerated whatever meaning he had had for her. Maybe she had come to the house just to look at it and by looking at it to understand just how much she had exaggerated the meaning she'd had for him, a meaning that had suddenly gone, whatever the meaning had been.

Yet she climbed the stairs, her footsteps the first to be made in the thin snow. The doorbell, she remembered, had no name under it, and she rang it. After a long wait, during which she thought she could hear the snow falling around her with a slight seething sound, she turned to descend, stepping in the footsteps she had made coming up. Halfway down, she heard the door open behind her, and she turned back to see an older man in what appeared to be a clerical

black cardigan standing in the doorway, a hall light lit behind him. Nancy climbed the stairs again to the man, who
wore large, gray felt slippers and had a soft, white face.

He said, quietly, "Come in out of the snow."

Nancy did, and in the hall of that silent house he looked
at her without asking what she wanted.

She said, "The last time I was here it was to see Aaron
Cohen."

"He's at the novitiate," the man said.

"Does that mean he's been baptized?"

"He has, yes, he has." The man had an Irish accent.

"So he'll become a monk?"

The man smiled weakly. "You could say that."

As Nancy was walking back through Central Park, a sudden
gust of wind made the snow whirl around her, and she felt
that this had some meaning: it appeared to her that everything had some meaning.

two

In Boston, Nancy turned Manos down the first few times he asked her to one of the Saturday night parties he often gave in the basement rumpus room of his parents' house, excusing herself, with a forced laugh, by saying she wasn't up to meeting his new girlfriend. He insisted that he didn't have a new girlfriend, but that though things were different between them, he still liked her company a lot. They went out on dates to a restaurant they had gone to when they were more of a couple, and sometimes they went to Symphony Hall for a concert or to a play, and when they parted Manos always kissed her on her cheek. She hesitated about going to his parties, but he persisted.

Soaking in her bathtub, up to her chin in foam, she raised her body up through the foam to look at it as she hadn't, it seemed to her, in a long time, or, maybe, not such a long time, but since she had stopped longing for Manos, or, better, stopped longing. The suds ran down between her breasts and slid from her thighs, and as she examined her body, long and thin and shining, she saw herself as a cadaver without thought or feeling or a soul, and then it occurred to her that Manos had once described dissecting the cadaver of an old man.

The telephone rang while she was drying herself, and she wrapped the large towel loosely about herself to go answer it. Manos invited her to a party that evening.

"I'm not going to give up on you," he said.

"Let's face it," she said, "you only want us to be friends because you feel guilty about our not being lovers. And I'm fine with it, believe me."

"That's not true, that's not at all true. I don't in the least feel guilty, not in the least. I just think that the best of our relationship was in the good times we had together."

"Meaning what? Not the good times we had in bed together?"

"Come on, Nancy, come on. My parents feel awful that you don't come, and are beginning to wonder if they're the reason why. They really like you. Come on."

"Maybe they'd like me more if I were Greek. Maybe you'd like me more if I were Greek."

"Let's not get into that, Nancy. If they were concerned that I was getting a little bit too serious with you, it wasn't because you're not Greek, but because they know I've got a long haul ahead of me at medical school that will need all the attention I can give it. And you know your not being Greek was never an issue for me."

"Nor, I suppose, my being a Jew was."

"You're offending me, Nan. You're really offending me."

"I'm sorry."

"So you'll come to the party," he said.

In fact, she did want to go to a party, so she said, "All right, all right, all right, have it your way."

"I'm inviting some interesting guys you've never met before."

Even though she had a paper due, Nancy spent most of the late early winter afternoon, the trees along the curbs now bare of leaves, shopping in Back Bay. She bought a long black sheath, sleeveless and without a waistline, that clung to her pelvis. She brushed her hair so it floated about her, and she wore no makeup on her thin, pale face except black eyeliner. Looking at herself in the full-length mirror on the back of her bathroom door, she thought she looked great.

She left her apartment to find that snow was falling, covering the steep sidewalks and streets of Beacon Hill. Her car was covered, and she had to brush off the windshield.

Driving to Brookline, Nancy told herself that, as a matter of fact, she really wasn't interested in Manos. And really never had been.

She parked the car behind a row of others along the curb and sat for a while to watch the snow drift down onto the windshield, and she thought of a forest filling with snow, no one there.

Her young body warm, she felt light walking over the snow-covered path to the front door. Manos opened the door and gave her a quick kiss. She put her hand on Manos's nape and squeezed it, drawing his head towards her, and kissed him more fully, to show him that she had gotten over him. This made him smile.

Abruptly, she went ahead of him into the entry hall, its floor covered with Oriental rugs, and as she went along the long, narrow hall she saw, through an arch, the living room, where more rugs, with red and dark blue and black geometrical designs and long fringes, overlapped one another.

"Where are your parents?" Nancy asked.

"Visiting relatives in Toronto."

"I thought they'd be waiting to welcome me with hugs and kisses."

"I'm sure they'd do just that if they were here, but they had to go visit family."

"Your people," Nancy said, "you're all over the world and all you ever see is one another."

The door to the rumpus room in the cellar was open, and from below voices swelled up.

"Am I the last one?" Nancy asked, descending.

"You wanted to be the last one."

"I did."

The low ceiling of the rumpus room was tiled in beige squares, the floor in brown and yellow squares, and in between the ceiling and the floor was a dark, cacophonous mass of people; around them were flashes of light. Nancy couldn't see into the mass, and she went to the bar, where Pam, whom she knew from college, and Pam's new boyfriend were sitting on bar stools.

Pam said, "I wish my folks would let me have a party when they go away."

"Why won't they?" Manos asked.

"Because they're Irish," Pam said, and hit her head; "Irish from Revere, and I'll have to live with that for the rest of my life."

"Are you Irish?" Nancy asked Pam's new boyfriend, whose name was Tony, and Nancy didn't know if that was Irish or not.

"I'm Italian," he said, "from Revere, which we pronounce Reveah."

"You look Irish."

Pam said, "If he was Irish, I wouldn't have anything to do with him."

Shaking the ice cubes in her glass, Nancy winked at Manos to thank him for the drink he'd given her, then wandered into the crowd. She'd spend as little time with Manos as possible.

Beyond a post, she saw Harry Stewart, a tall, lanky, black friend from BU, talking with a guy she didn't know.

The stranger she didn't know was wearing a white dress shirt, the sleeves rolled up to his elbows, and his fingers were pressed to his chest. It was his hands that Nancy noticed—they were large, with long fingers and big knuckles, and they had small knobs at the base of the thumbs. Very masculine hands. But the guy's neck, revealed by his open collar, which looked too big for him, was slender, and he looked as though he'd hardly begun to shave.

For all her forwardness, Nancy was in fact shy, or so she told herself. She looked at the guy with the man's hands and the boy's face for a moment, then went back to Manos and, indicating the guy with her glass, asked, "Who's he?"

She remembered that she'd asked Vinnie the same thing about Aaron.

"Yvon."

"Yvon?

"Yes."

"What's his last name?"

" Gendreau."

"What kind of name is that?"

"French."

"He's from France?"

"No, he's American. French-American."

"I've never met a French-American."

"Now's your chance."

Nancy wrinkled her nose at Manos, as if to reproach him for the liberty he was giving her to take up with anyone she wanted to.

Adding to the reproach, she said, "He's sort of sexy."

"That's for you to say," Manos said, "not me."

"You don't think he's sexy?"

"If I were a woman, I suppose I'd have some fantasies about his big-man hands." This sounded like something Vinnie would say.

"I'm a woman, and, you know what, I think it's not just his big masculine hands, it's his hands and his boy's face that give me a little turn."

Manos put his arms around Nancy's waist and drew her to him to hug her closely, but she pushed him away, pressing her glass against his chest.

"You're jealous," she said.

"Sure I am."

She said, "Take me over to Yvon and introduce me; you bragged to me about inviting interesting guys."

"You go," Manos said.

"But I'm shy."

"Overcoming your shyness makes you the most forward person in the world. You go."

Nancy pressed her glass harder against his chest. "I'm telling you, you don't want to introduce me to him because you are jealous."

Manos grabbed the glass pressed to his chest, drank from

it, and gave it back to her. "Go," he said, "go try to find out if any guy can be better than I am. Go see if Yvon's the guy." Manos turned away.

But she was shy, and her shyness, she thought, made her conscious of herself as she moved toward Harry and Yvon, feeling the cloth of her dress cling to her hips. She tried to look as if she was wandering; as she approached she exclaimed, "Hey, Harry," and she quickly reached for one of Harry's hands and swung it so he laughed and said, "Nancy," and he added, "babe," and she smiled and said, "Babe to you, but only to you." Then she turned to Yvon and said "Sorry, I interrupted what you were saying."

Before Yvon could speak, Harry said, "This guy here was trying to tell me I'm wrong."

Nancy asked Yvon, "How is Harry wrong?"

And Yvon, confronted, stepped back. "I didn't say he's wrong. I wouldn't say that."

It was not very original of him, Nancy thought, and her first impression of Yvon was that he was not very original, but it didn't matter.

Harry said, "Look, a president points at me and tells me not to ask what the country can do for me, but what I can do for the country. You tell me, what have I ever gotten from a country where I have to think of myself first, because the country is out to defeat me in everything I do? This guy doesn't understand that."

Nancy said to Yvon, "So?"

"I was trying to say that we're all Americans," Yvon said, his blue eyes wide.

"Sure, sure," Harry said, "we're all Americans," and

he moved his neck back and forth, and his shoulders, hips, knees, and feet moved as if he were doing a little dance, and he danced away from Nancy and Yvon.

Yvon stood still, embarrassed, and Nancy, too, was embarrassed, though she didn't know why. She noted the way Yvon's sideburns ended not at a razor-sharp edge but in fine points, and his round, smooth jaw. She was shy about looking at him in the eyes, but she did to ask, abruptly, "Manos told me your last name, but I forgot it."

He said, "Gendreau. Yvon Gendreau."

"So where do you live, Yvon Gendreau?"

"I'm sharing a room in BU housing near the campus."

"An undergraduate?" she asked, and she thought: a boy.

"Yes, I'm an undergraduate, a senior," establishing credentials for being at a party of graduate students.

"How'd you get here?"

"My roommate has a car."

"Where is he?"

"He left." Yvon frowned to check a smile. By the way he tried to check his smile, she knew he had come to this party to pick someone up. "And he has the car."

"Nice guy, your roommate."

"He left with somebody."

Stepping away from him, Nancy said, "When you want to leave, let me know and I'll give you a lift," and she turned away.

Couples were dancing. Manos was dancing with a coed, and as Nancy passed them, Manos lifted his cheek from the coed's cheek and winked at her. On the other side of the dance floor, she saw, through the dancing couples, Yvon Gendreau, where she had left him.

He appeared to be staring, unblinking, at no one. He's a loner, Nancy thought, oh yes, a lonely loner.

This came to her: she'd offer to leave now. The thought—more a sensation—roused in her a sense of daring.

When the record ended and the couples stopped dancing, she went right to Yvon Gendreau and said, "Look, I'm going. If you want to go, too, I'll give you that lift I promised."

He looked beyond her, just for a moment, then looked at her, and said, "Thanks."

She drew back, momentarily unsure whether she should invite him into her car, but she said, "My name's Nancy, Nancy Green."

He nodded.

And she heard herself say, "So, do you want a ride?"

"You want to give me a ride?"

"I wouldn't have offered a ride if I didn't."

It was as if they were alone, the two of them, and the party disappeared. With a sudden, unexpected, wide smile, Yvon Gendreau said, "I'd like to come with you."

And now she felt that he all too easily said he'd go with her, as if he expected something that she, after all, wasn't sure she wanted to give to this unknown loner.

He followed her upstairs to the entry where the coats were piled on the floor, and after he politely helped her on with hers, he put on his parka. Snow was still falling, and they stood on the flagstone stoop looking at it.

She said, "Come on."

In the car, she didn't ask where he wanted her to give him a lift to, and he didn't say. She drove into Boston along Commonwealth Avenue. It was by now a dark winter Saturday morning and she drove around the center of the city, stopping at red lights in streets with no traffic but her car, and she parked on Beacon Street by the Common.

The illuminated lamps on posts in the snow-covered Common looked like bare trees in a landscape of low hills. The falling snow was visible in the light of the lamps, but not in the darkness beyond the light.

Nancy opened her door and got out. Yvon hesitated before he got out on his side. He followed her into the Common. Snow-filled wind blew about them. They walked under bare trees, the branches shining white in the lamps that cast their shadows on the ground. Along the path were fence-high iron posts with chains slung between them. Beyond the chains was the bank-side of a hill, and in the snow on the bank was a bunch of roses. Yvon reached over the chain and picked them up by the green tissue paper wrapped round the stems, and, holding the bouquet high, said, "Look, how beautiful." This unexpected remark struck her as odd, and odd, too, was the pleasure she took from its very oddity. Bowing from the waist, he chivalrously held the bouquet out to her, and she, smiling with pleasure, took it. He didn't smile.

Seeming ready to go wherever she went, he walked behind Nancy as she led him from Beacon Street up Beacon Hill to the old brick building where she lived. Petals dropped from the roses as she took Yvon up dim stairs, unlocked her door, and led him now into the large room with a double bed. The old-fashioned gas streetlamp outside the wide, many-paned, curtain-less window lit the room. Nancy did not turn on a light inside. She placed the roses on the mantelpiece.

* * *

Yvon removed his parka and sat on the edge of the bed on the far side from her. She let her coat drop to the floor, kicked off her shoes, and lay on the bed. Lying full length and combing out her damp hair with her fingers, Nancy watched him lie down beside her.

Placing her hand lightly across his throat, she said, "So you're French-American."

"We say Franco, Franco-American."

"What's it like to be Franco-American?"

"You really want to know?"

"Won't you tell me?" she asked.

His lips expanded into a smile, as if his lips were always about to expand into a smile.

Though she wanted to make love with him, it would be all right if they didn't, if they just lay together on the bed. And if he did want to, she wouldn't be the one to start, she wouldn't try to get him to do something he didn't want to do. She even wished he'd continue simply to lie beside her on the bed.

Slowly, he took her hand in his and brought it, palm down, to cover his smile, and as he pressed it to his lips he licked her palm. A little shock went through her, and, laughing, she tried to pull her hand away. But he held it more tightly to lick her palm again, while she, laughing from the shock, again tried to yank her hand away. He held her wrist in both his hands and she now felt that her entire body was in his hand, and when he bit her on the pad below her thumb she yelled and laughed. Then she saw him staring up at her from the side of her hand, his eyes shining, and she stopped laughing. He let go of her to reach out, with his wide-open palms, for her head, which he held tightly.

"What do you want?" she asked.

He didn't kiss her, but, holding her head more tightly, brought his lips close to hers, and when she strained forward to kiss him he held her head back, and stared at her.

"What do you want?" she asked again.

"I want to make love with you," he said.

She tried to draw back, but he held her. "What love?"

"The most wonderful." He brushed his lips against her, lightly, and whispered, "Oh, the most wonderful."

But his intensity shocked her. "Let me go," she insisted.

He did and again they lay side by side.

She should tell him to leave, but she didn't. She asked, "And why do you think making love with me would be so wonderful?"

He suddenly jumped up and off the bed, his body against the dim light from the window like a shadow, and he raised his arms high and said, "Because I want all that's most wonderful in the world."

She studied him, then said, "Well, okay," because for him making wonderful love was a boy's fantasy, and she'd allow him his fantasy.

She had never before made love as she did now with Yvon, never before. The bedclothes were twisted about them by their twisting and turning, and nighttime cold drafts blew cold against their bodies in their, to her, wonderful love making.

The central heating came on, and the cast-iron radiator

in the corner of the room hissed. Lying propped up side by side with pillows against the headboard of the bed, he, his arm behind her back, played with her hair, twirling strands together, curling it round his fingers, gathering it up loosely and letting it drop on her bare shoulders.

"Are all Franco-Americans like you?"

"All."

"Take your pillow away and lie back," Nancy said, and when he did she rose and straddled him and began to massage his shoulders. His body seemed to be in part that of a boy, in part that of a man. His delicate clavicles were a boy's, his shoulders a man's. His man's chest was as hairless as a boy's. His thighs were a boy's, as were the smooth grooves of his groin, but the rest of him there was certainly a man. She told him to turn over onto his stomach, and she pressed her fingers into his nape, over his shoulders, along his spine. He became so still, so still and so silent, she asked, "Are you all right?" He remained still and silent, and then, laughing, he turned over to face her.

He ran his hands over her back, her thighs, her buttocks, and, again, the shock occurred: never before had she made love as she did with this man. They lay together wrapped in sheets and blankets, the darkness about them filled with dawn light, and in it the snow falling outside appeared to be falling in the room.

"Shouldn't we get up?" she asked.

"No."

"Then tell me about being French."

"Franco."

"You come from French Canada?"

"Not me. My ancestors did. I come from a small Franco parish in Providence, Rhode Island."

"A parish? What's that? It sounds like a village far away and from a long, long time ago."

"It is. It's where I was born and brought up."

"Do you go back?"

"Every weekend. It's where I should be now. I'll be leaving here to go there by an early train."

"Your parents expect you?"

"My mother does."

"She lives alone?"

"She lives with my older, bachelor brother."

"Why haven't I ever heard of Francos?"

"We're not known." He held up his hands on either side of his face and grimaced. "We're ghosts," he said, and he dropped his hands and laughed.

He was joking, but his joking startled Nancy. As if to assert her self-control against the loss of control she felt, she placed a hand between her breasts, she said, "I'm Jewish. I guess we're well enough known for you to have heard of us."

"I've heard of you."

And with a reassuring thrill of pleasure, she thought again that never, ever before had she ever made love with someone whom she was so drawn to as Yvon.

She felt that he was pulling her out to some area beyond the bed, beyond the room, out into the dark, as if what he was doing was more than having sex, but struggling with her to make a ghost of her, while still and silent people formed a circle about them and watched.

He turned to lie slackly on her, and she felt his breath on her neck, she felt his heart beating. She kept her arms on either side of him, as though to hold him would be more than she could now bear of the weight of his body.

He whispered, "Wonderful."

And she said, "Yes, wonderful."

While he was in the bathtub, she remained in bed, dozing. He came in dressed but with his hair still wet and said he had to go.

"My mother will be waiting for me."

Nancy didn't want to hear about Yvon's mother, or why she was waiting for him.

"Lie down beside me for a minute before you go," she said.

He did, gathering her up, she felt, in his large, warm, and, as she now thought, peasant hands.

"When can I see you again?" she asked.

"Well, during the week I've got my classes and my studies and I have a job."

All she wanted to know about him was when she would see him again. She said, "Come and have some dinner with me next Sunday."

He asked, "Is that possible?"

"Why shouldn't it be possible?"

"I mean, you really want me to?"

"I want you to."

He put on his sweater and parka and scarf and gloves, and Nancy got up and pulled a sheet from the bed and drew it about herself to go to the door of the apartment with him. She watched him go down the stairs to the street door, where, the door open onto the snow, he turned back to her for a moment.

The bathroom smelled a little of what she took to be his smell, mingled in the scented steam that rose from the bath salts she had poured into the hot, deep water. His smell was like that of wood smoke.

Over the week, the roses on the mantelpiece dried and withered and turned black. Nancy thought of keeping them, perhaps just the petals in a sachet bag, but reconsidered: she must not be sentimental about someone she'd just met. She threw the roses away.

But Sunday afternoon she waited for him, from time to time looking out the window. Snow was falling. She was looking when the downstairs bell rang.

He arrived with his little valise—an old, khaki military valise: he had come directly from the train station.

"I hope I'm not imposing," he said.

She laughed and held out her arms to him. She wanted him to impose on her.

He was covered in snow, his hair, his eyebrows and eyelashes, the shoulders and sleeves of his parka, and his shoes had become encased in larger shoes of impacted snow. She helped him off with his parka and shook it as he shook his head and stomped his shoes. Melted snow puddled on the wooden floor. She threw his parka on a chair and stood in the puddle to put her arms around him and kiss him.

His body, in bed, seemed to her to exhale the freshness of snow, then, when the blood heated it, the muskiness of wood smoke.

She cooked him a meal on the old gas stove, and, as they ate at the maplewood drop-leaf table in the kitchen, she asked about his parish, where he had just come from, which she thought of as far, far away, maybe deep in a snowbound forest. But he seemed not interested enough to tell her about his parish.

From his valise he took out what looked like a huge, jagged crystal and held it out to her and said, "I brought this to give to you."

She took it in both hands and lifted it to her eyes. "What is it?"

"It's quartz, from my collection of rocks and minerals."

The quartz was in part opaque, in part with layers upon translucent layers.

"You have a collection?"

"I have a collection of all kinds of stones, from granite to quartz. I like the stones embedded with mica best, I guess, because the mica sparkles in the rough black stone."

Nancy said, "You love beautiful things."

He shook his head, as if she must not take him seriously, and yet he said, "I do, I do."

"Well, thank you." She stared again into the quartz, and suddenly wondered why Yvon had given it to her. She said, a little surprised, "It really is beautiful."

"Even more so if you hold it up to the light."

She did, against the sudden winter bright rays through the dirty window, and it refracted the light.

"Do you like it?" Yvon asked.

"I do."

"Really?"

"Really."

"I'm not imposing it on you?"

"Imposing it on me?"

"I worry that I'm imposing on you. Am I? Am I demanding too much?"

"You don't seem to me to demand anything," she said.

She didn't know where to put the quartz crystal: she felt it needed a special place, one he would recognize as special, one he would recognize as her finding him special. She looked about the room, and, drawn through the rays of late sunlight, went to the window and set the quartz on the lower windowsill, where it refracted the light brilliantly. She returned to where Yvon stood and together they looked at the brilliantly refracted light. She reached out an arm and placed it over his shoulders, and this gave him all the permission he needed to pull her closer to him, raise the palm of her hand to his lips so that it contorted her arm with a flash of pain, but the pain gave her a sense of the reality of his passion. He bit into the flesh of her palm under her thumb, then he said, "I want so much."

Nancy drew her hand away, apprehensive about what Yvon wanted from her, and to deflect him from whatever that was she asked, "How's your mother?"

"Oh," he said, and shrugged, and she understood that he didn't want to talk about his mother.

"And your brother?"

"He's taking care of my mother."

Pressing him, she asked, "Your mother needs to be taken care of?"

He wouldn't be pressed beyond saying, "I go every weekend to help my brother do just that."

All right, she thought, he wouldn't talk about his mother. She asked, "That's everything he does, he takes care of your mother?"

"He has a small printing business in the parish."

"What's his name?"

"Cyriac."

"Is that a Franco name?"

Yvon laughed. "It isn't Irish or Italian or Polish."

"Well," she said, "tell me something about your parish."

"A story?"

"I'd like a story."

"Let me think." He put a hand over his forehead while he thought, and, thinking, seemed to try to laugh. "I want to tell you a funny story, a story that'll make you laugh."

"Tell me."

"Here's one," he said, "a story my grandmother used to tell me. She made medicine from sumac berries she collected, and, without her knowing it, once the medicine fermented it became really potent, and everyone in the parish, even the pastor of the parish church, kept coming to her for a bottle to cure illnesses none of them had."

"Where did your grandmother learn to make a medicine from sumac berries?"

"From her mother. My grandmother was an Indian, Micmac."

"So you're part Indian."

"Most Francos are."

"So are the people in your parish a kind of tribe?"

"A kind of, I suppose."

"It sounds far away."

"Oh," he said, "very far away."

But she knew it wasn't really that far if it was in Providence, a short train ride away.

Before he came to bed that night, he stood by the window and looked out. He looked out, she thought, at the gas lamp on the street and the snow wheeling around it. She lay quietly, waiting for him to turn and come. He was wearing only a tee shirt, so half his buttocks were exposed. Getting into bed, he reached out to her.

He tickled her, licked her ears, played with her hair, and interlaced her fingers in complicated ways with his. And then, as if love making were everything in the world he must have, he became passionate.

At night the steam heat in the apartment was turned off, and, asleep, they held each other. When at times she awoke because she was cold and found him, in the light from the streetlamp through the window, lying apart from her, his eyes open, she'd look at him for a while before moving over to him and putting her arm about his waist, and he'd close his eyes.

Through November and December, during which the snow deepened, froze over, and deepened more, he came to her every Sunday afternoon on his return by train from Providence to Boston. They didn't see each other over the week. Even though they were at the same university, he was an undergraduate majoring in French and she a graduate studying for a master's in English, and that made a big difference between them. Nancy thought, also, that maybe

she preferred seeing him only on Sunday afternoons, right
from his parish. Maybe she preferred having him separate
from the rest of her life, in which she went out with friends
for a meal or for drinks at a place called My Place Or Your
Place. All week, she looked forward to Sunday, the earlier
the better.

The next time she asked about his parish he told her a
story about an old woman named Eva Lajoie who visited
everyone in the parish, just walked in on them. She had
bulging breasts and hair on her chin, and she was known for
farting fits that she tried to control by holding her breath
and going rigid. Everyone knew she was having a fit when
she stopped talking and held her breath and went rigid.
She always had a lot to tell, about the sick and dying, about
wakes and funerals. Madame LeBlanc's cancer was coming
out all over her body in bleeding sores, Monsieur Levesque
had sat up just before he died and shouted "Tabernacle!" at
his wife.

Nancy stopped him. What did "tabernacle" mean?

It meant where the consecrated host was kept in church,
and it was the worst, most blaspheming word you could say
in Franco.

She told him to go on.

Madame Dandeneau's son was drunk at her wake, and
Madame Legrand had asked in her will for a High Mass
for her funeral but her daughters paid for only a Low Mass.
It wasn't for this gossip that Eva Lajoie was welcomed by
everyone, but for the fits and the fart, which always came
after she had thought the fit was over and she breathed out
and relaxed. Yvon remembered her talking about her pre-

monitions—people in the parish were always having pre-monitions—of her own death.

"What happened to her?" Nancy asked.

"Her premonitions were fulfilled," he said. "She died."

Nancy didn't know if she should laugh at this or not, and only did when Yvon did.

He came back from Providence one late afternoon and said nothing about the parish, maybe because he thought she'd heard enough. She hadn't heard enough. She thought that maybe he felt his stories were no longer funny, and unless he could make them funny he shouldn't tell them. Or, she thought, maybe he was low and felt he couldn't tell her anything that would make her laugh. She wanted him to be spirited, as he always was when his enthusiasm about what he was saying animated his face, his hands, all his body.

While they were eating, she asked him, "Don't you have a story for me?" She wanted to raise his spirits and also to find out more about him, because, for all the stories he told her about his parish, she still had no idea, no idea at all, where he came from or who he was.

He sighed, then said, "I went to a wake on Friday evening and a funeral Saturday morning."

"Oh."

"What about your weekend?"

"I saw Manos," she said.

"He gave a party?"

"He took me to a party given by a friend of his, in Brookline, where I didn't know anyone."

"I didn't think not knowing anyone would stop you from knowing anyone you wanted to know."

She smiled. "I didn't want to know anyone."

She washed the dishes and he dried, both silent, and both thinking. She was thinking of him, but she had no idea what he was thinking.

She asked, "Are there any Jews in your parish, any at all?"

"Jews in the parish?" he exclaimed. "I didn't even know there were Jews in Providence, or Boston, or all of New England. Jews live only in New York."

"That's me—a Jew from New York."

He laughed. "That's what you are—a Jew from New York."

"And what does that mean to you?"

"I don't know," he said.

As she was clearing the table, he took from her the two plates she held and placed them back on the table and put his arms around her.

"Please," he asked, "can we go to bed?"

She smiled. "You're tired?"

Smiling back, he said, "No, not tired, not in any way tired."

"Lonely?" He pressed his forehead against hers.

In bed, he grabbed her and pulled her to him and almost chanted, "Oh, I want, I want, I want—"

He was hurting her so she dug her nails into his shoulders and he let go. He rolled away onto his side. She reached out and held him. He pressed his face into the side of her neck, and she rocked him a little in her arms.

* * *

They began to meet during the week on campus between classes, and she sometimes cut a class to meet him. He would not cut a class; his duty to his studies would not allow him even though she tried to make fun of him for just this: his sense of duty. She knew, absolutely, that he did not date anyone else, and would have been shocked if she did. She didn't. She might make fun, lightly, about his sense of duty, but she liked it for the reassurance it gave her. She had no doubts about him, none.

He always waited for her to invite him to her apartment; he wouldn't presume to take going there for granted. Leaving her on campus to return to his room to study— he must go to his room to study—she would say, "See you later," which was not quite enough of an invitation; he'd ask, "What time?" and, as always, he rang her bell at just that time. Again, she'd joke with him that he was, oh, so very polite, and should appear whenever he wanted, but she was also reassured by this politeness, this courteousness. She joked about his chivalrousness—opening a door for her, carrying her books, walking on the outside on the sidewalk, bringing small gifts of postcard reproductions of works of art—but all this also reassured her. And in her apartment he respected her private life; she knew he would never ask who telephoned her while they were together, who were the friends whom she saw on her own, whom she had slept with, though he must have known about Manos.

But for all this reserve, when they were together making love he was, amazingly, without reserve. Their love making could start up suddenly, as if the potential of it were a constant in the slightly steamy heat of the apartment, and his smallest gesture—yanking off his tie and unbuttoning his collar, pulling her hair back from her face and letting it fall, a smile—would provoke larger, violent gestures of their whole bodies.

She was preparing tomato sauce for pasta. He came into the kitchen. He sucked sauce from her fingers, and, leaving the sauce in the pot, they spent the evening and night and dawn in bed, and all her body was tinglingly chafed by his light beard.

He always left in the morning to return to his room, especially if he were studying for an exam.

At the beginning of Christmas break, she drove him to Providence on her way to New York. Though she said she would take him all the way to his parish, he insisted no, she shouldn't, he could take a bus from the train station.

"Where is your parish?" she asked. "Is it far from downtown?"

"It's far enough that you'd go at least an hour out of your way."

"That's all right with me."

"No," he repeated.

He probably didn't want her to see his parish, and she assumed he didn't because it was a poor place, because he knew she came from a wealthier place. But he seemed unaware of the signs that marked him as poor: his frayed plaid shirts, a sweater with a hole in the elbow, his old army valise. Whatever it was he didn't want her to see, which had to be more than that the parish was poor, she couldn't insist on going there, she couldn't make him show her what he didn't want to.

High banks of snow had been plowed up around the train station to form a snowscape with cars, among which Nancy stopped.

Yvon remained sitting next to her.

"You're sure you won't let me take you to your parish?"

Reaching for the door handle, he said, "I am," but, his arm bent at an odd angle, again he became still.

He didn't want her to go with him, and he didn't, she realized, want to go alone.

He said, "I was thinking of spending the break in my room in Boston, but then thought I couldn't, really—"

"Because of your mother?"

He drew in his breath.

"Listen," Nancy said, "I'm going to give you a set of keys to my apartment, so that whenever you want to get away you can go there." She took the set from the glove compartment, and he held out his hand for it, then, as before, sat still beside her.

She thought, he doesn't want to leave me, and this thought filled her with a tender desire to take him with her, take him wherever she went. A small urge came to her just to drive off with him now. She felt that he wouldn't object, and that for her to drive off with him was what he was waiting for.

He pressed the door handle down and opened the door, but, instead of turning to go, he turned more toward her and put his arms around her, and then he lurched sideways away from her, getting out of the car quickly.

As she pulled away, she saw him in her rearview mirror standing near a snowbank, his valise at his side, and she stopped, turned the ignition off, but remained where she was in the car, looking at Yvon in the rearview mirror. He hadn't moved, as if he had no choice but to stay where he was. On impulse, somewhere beyond making a choice, she opened the car door and, shaking her head so her hair flew out, she strode to him and said, "I'm taking you to your parish. Get in the car."

Which he did, talking only to direct her up a hill along an avenue of tenements, and into a side street of clapboard bungalows, all heavy with snow. The side street was icy, and when he said, "You can stop here," the car skidded a little. Nancy parked the car at a deep snowbank, and beyond the bank was a small gray clapboard bungalow with a narrow porch supported by pillars, icicles hanging from the edge of the porch's roof gutter. Yvon did not move.

Nancy said, "Come on."

He did everything she said, as if coming here had all been up to her, not him, and he followed her through a path in the snowdrift and up the stairs to the porch, but she stood aside when he rang a bell by the storm door.

Nancy was apprehensive. The ice around the storm door cracked and the door slowly opened, and she felt a flash of fear. The door opened to a thin, taut woman in a housedress and a heavy cardigan that was too big for her, and, as if she couldn't quite see, she frowned when she recognized her son, then frowned again when Yvon stepped aside for his mother to see Nancy.

"I'm Nancy."

"I know."

"You know?"

"Yvon told me," his mother said, and, as if she had expected Nancy, she led the way into the living room of large, overstuffed armchairs and sofa and a cedar chest in the middle, all in the dim snow light, and the room was winter cold.

Nancy noted that the short, graying hair of Yvon's mother looked as if it had been cut with large shears, maybe by herself. Silent, Mrs. Gendreau went ahead of Nancy and Yvon and opened a door into the kitchen, then shut the door to keep the kitchen warm. The floor was covered with worn linoleum patterned with the heads of clowns and merry-go-rounds and Ferris wheels. The room was crowded, with a large range and an old refrigerator and a high-backed rocking chair and a table with chairs around it, and what might have been a seventeenth-century cabinet with the marks of an adze on its thick wood sides. Yvon's mother gestured to Nancy to take off her coat, and hung the coat in a closet in which Nancy saw a broom, a snow shovel, and what looked like a sheep's pelt hanging among other coats. Yvon threw his parka onto a chair, as though to show he and Nancy would not stay long.

Nancy felt that she had never been in a place as strange as this, had never met a woman as strange as Yvon's mother, who put a kettle to boil on the range.

As if daring herself, Nancy said, "Yvon told you about me?"

But instead of answering her, Yvon's mother spoke to him in French. She spoke with what had to be a Franco accent, a rough accent new to Nancy, which Yvon had clearly taught himself not to reflect in English. Nancy couldn't understand any of the French of mother and son, but then Yvon told his mother to speak English, and she said nothing, and didn't look at Nancy.

No, Nancy thought, there was nothing for her here in this strangeness, and nothing here would reveal to her something about Yvon she had wanted to know. She wanted to leave; she wanted to leave Yvon behind and go on to New York.

With an old key, Yvon's mother opened the old cabinet for mugs, a box of tea bags, a bowl of sugar, and spoons and little plates and a narrow box of cookies, all of which she placed silently on the wooden table with a bottle of milk from the refrigerator. She appeared to act as though she were alone.

Yvon said to Nancy, "There's a lot of history in that cabinet."

He was pointing out to her the antique cabinet, the only evidence in the house of something to be proud of, the only claim he had to any value in his long history, a long history, Nancy suddenly felt, without value to her.

Hanging above the cabinet was a framed oleograph of Christ holding open his red robe to reveal a bloody heart and looking up with an expression of suffering endured because he had no choice but to suffer, and this image appeared stark to Nancy, the image of a stark religion, the stark religion of Yvon's mother, of Yvon, of the parish.

And the single impression Nancy had of Yvon's mother was of hard starkness. She has, Nancy thought, the small black eyes of an Indian.

And Yvon's eyes were blue.

Yvon stared at Nancy as though with the nervous antici-
pation of her reaction with at least some interest in the old
cabinet, and Nancy smiled at him, as if to let him know she
understood, with a little echo of pity for him here in this
house, here with his mother.

His mother indicated a chair for Nancy to sit at the
wooden table, and when Yvon and his mother sat his mother poured boiling water into mugs with tea bags in them
and slowly opened the box of cookies.

She again spoke briefly to Yvon in French, and again
Yvon insisted on English, but, suddenly, instead of speaking, she rapped her knuckles against the edge of the table.

Yvon looked at Nancy, worried by what she would make
of this, but in his look was a plea to her not to worry.

His mother rapped the edge of the table with her knuckles more and more violently, and Nancy worried about what
this meant. She stood and said to Yvon, "I'd better go now."

He didn't speak, but his mother turned to Nancy, the
palms of her hands held out as if as an offering of herself, and she said, "I'm sorry," and Nancy saw how tense her
gaunt face was.

And though she had no idea what Yvon's mother was
apologizing for, and not knowing what else to say, Nancy
said, "Oh, don't be sorry."

"All I want," Mrs. Gendreau said, "is for my son to be
happy. I can't make him happy. You do that, you make him
happy."

"Ma," Yvon said, and then he spoke to his mother in
French, which, his expression conveyed, was meant to stop

her from talking. Leaving the cups of tea and the cookies on the table, Yvon quickly took Nancy's coat from the closet, helped her put it on, and, without his parka, showed her to a back door that opened into the outside cold, and he walked with her to where her car was parked at the front of the house. Nancy understood that Yvon had brought her into the house by the front door because that was the visitors' door to enter and out the back door because she was no longer a visitor.

At the car, she reached out and held him closely to her, and he let her hold him.

She said, "Your poor mother."

He said, "My mother."

She rubbed his arms through his shirtsleeves to warm him a little before he left her to get into her car.

As Nancy drove, her concentration on the highway seemed to converge on a point always ahead of her. How could she ever understand Yvon in his world, and the world he lived in with his mother? If she saw Yvon's mother as helpless, so, too, must Yvon be, for when his mother, as if praying, said that all she wanted for her son was his happiness, Nancy knew that the mother's prayer wouldn't be answered, that both mother and son could never be happy in the world they lived in, a cold, dark, snowbound world, their native world, a world so unknown to Nancy that she would never understand why she was as attracted to Yvon as she was.

The green interstate sign for New York appeared to emerge from the green light of the highway lamps, and then to pass into space behind her.

She knew her parents were expecting her, and she wanted to be with them.

In Manhattan, she drove through slush, swerving in it when she braked at red lights. Outside, people appeared black and remote against the lit stores.

She parked her car in a side street off Fifth Avenue. A doorman she didn't know opened the door to the apartment building for her, and she had to explain she was the daughter of Mr. and Mrs. Green.

They were waiting to have dinner with her.

Nancy's father, as always, did most of the talking, and, as always, Nancy didn't know for certain if her mother listened or not, but whenever her father stopped talking her mother asked, "What were you saying?"

Wondering about Yvon with his mother, Nancy listened and didn't listen to her father. She thought: I'm not interested in Yvon, let him take care of his crazy mother.

During dinner she hardly spoke, and, because she always had a lot to recount whenever she came back from Boston, her father asked, "Are you all right?" and when she said, "I'm all right," her mother, after another silence, asked her, "Are you all right?" and again she said, "Like I said, yes." She knew that her parents worried about her because of her moods, but she had learned to assure them that she no longer gave in to her moods, and she didn't, because she no longer had those moods. After dinner, her mother asked her if she was going to go out, and she said she hadn't thought about it. "You mean," her father asked, laughing, "you're going to stay in?" She tried to laugh, answering, "I only said I hadn't thought about it." She didn't want to telephone anyone, though to telephone someone was always the first thought she had in the past when she returned to New York from Boston. She didn't really want to see anyone, not even Vinnie.

She went to her room and lay on her bed, the lights off.

But her mother came in and, moving slowly in the dark, switched on a light by Nancy's bed.

Nancy sat up. "You want to talk to me?"

"Just to ask how you are in Boston."

"I'm fine."

"How's Manos?"

"He's fine."

"You don't spend too much time in Boston lying on your bed in a darkened room?"

"Don't worry about that. I have a lot of studying to do."

'How is that going?"

"Interesting."

"You know how much we want you to be happy."

"I know, I know. But maybe you want that too much for me."

"Too much?"

"As if you're a little scared that I'm getting into one of my moods."

"We do think about that."

"And you both feel that's happening?"

"I suppose Dr. Quinn alerted us to any signs, not that that's for anyone to say but you."

"I like to think Dr. Quinn is way in the past. I'm over Dr. Quinn, who was long enough ago that I can deal with a mood when I feel it coming on. Just now, I was a little tired, so I thought I'd rest, that's all."

"Then I'll let you rest," her mother said, but as she reached out to switch off the lamp, Nancy said, "Leave it on, I'll do some reading."

Her mother leaned over and kissed her on the forehead before going out.

But Nancy didn't have the concentration to read, though, lying still, she kept the lamp lit.

Out on a solitary morning walk around the reservoir in Central Park, she thought of Aaron Cohen, thought of him as someone whom she, at the very back of her mind, was sometimes still thinking about. She could not imagine where he was, if he was anywhere in the world, and maybe it was just because she could not imagine him anywhere in this world that he remained a shadow within the shadows of another world at the back of her mind. For a moment, she considered going to the house where he had lived to ask someone where he was, but then she felt she didn't want to know. She told herself he was not so important that she should know.

On Christmas day, the Greens went to visit a cousin named Gil and his wife Maria and their withdrawn son, Adam, whose long hair was rolled into dreadlocks; he kept to himself. Looking at the tree, lit up with candles in old-fashioned candleholders, Maria, who had converted from Catholicism to Judaism although Gil was not a practicing Jew, said, "I call it a Hanukkah bush," and Nancy said, the words separate and hard, "Please spare me."

* * *

When she returned to her apartment in Boston, she found, across the back of a chair near the bed, one of Yvon's shirts. It had not been there when she left. She thought he might have moved in and was living there, and, out now, would be back at any moment. She waited for him, going from time to time to the window. Snowbanks were higher than ever along the curbs.

Because Yvon had a key to the apartment, when the bell rang downstairs on Sunday evening Nancy wondered who was there. Yvon always came in the afternoon, and she thought that maybe he had stayed in his parish with his mother. But then she thought he was too polite to come in on her without letting her know beforehand. She hurried down the stairs. He stood in the light of the hissing gas lamp with his old army valise, and, the door open to the street, she hugged him as if she had worried that she might never see him again. She asked, "Are you all right?"

He said, "I am now that I'm with you."

Upstairs, even before he took off his parka, she, unable to help herself, pulled at him, hugged him and kissed him, and they fell onto the bed.

In the after-midnight silence, Nancy woke, and, about to switch off the lamp by the bed, she saw Yvon raise his head, his eyes closed, and reach out for her. She lowered herself so his hand grasped her shoulder. Asleep, he kissed her shoulder, the side of her neck, her cheek and temple, and as he slowly kissed her he curled a hand into a loose fist and pressed it between her breasts.

* * *

After Yvon left her in the morning to return for the week to his room in the student apartment house near BU, Nancy, putting a little order in the disorder of her apartment, found one of his socks by the bed. He kept a drawer of socks and underclothes in her apartment. Partly because she wanted him to be with her so she could make sure he was all right, and also because she wanted him to share her bed night after night—maybe she wanted him to share her bed with her night after night to make sure he was all right—she wished he would move in with her. When he next came, she hinted at this, telling him she was going to get rid of a lot of clothes and that would leave space in her closet, but, not quite certain what she meant, he smiled. He was not good at picking up hints.

She said, "I'm asking you to live with me."

"I think I'd offend my Irish roommate if I left him."

"Are you real friends?"

"I try to be to him, but I don't think he is to me."

"Well," Nancy said, "if you want to come and live here we can move your things in my car."

His eyes large, with the expression of a boy committing himself to something he must show her he was capable of committing himself to, he said, "Only if I pay half the rent."

She tapped his cheek and said, "Never mind that."

"Only if I do," he said.

He couldn't, she was sure, pay half the rent; he hardly had enough money from his brother Cyriac and his job in a university cafeteria, and, too, he had a university loan to pay for tuition and his room and board, but he insisted. She said, "All right." But she would pay and not tell him, and she would accept if he forgot, because he couldn't pay.

Seeing his shirt hanging over the back of a chair, his loose change on the top of the bureau in the bedroom, his razor on the shelf under the mirror of the medicine cabinet in the bathroom, she felt a little better about him.

And she very much liked being in bed together for the night, when the sheets, the blankets, the pillows seemed to be part of their warm intimacy, and it also seemed to her that the intimacy deepened as, awake just enough to talk, they would slowly fall asleep.

The light of the street streetlamp through the many-paned window cast the shadows of the frames on the bed where they lay, Nancy's head on Yvon's chest, her long hair spread out.

He was talking to her about his course in French literature, which, he said, made him consider the long history of the French he was brought up with. He said, "My mother speaks what she calls the French French she was taught by nuns in the parish school, and I was, too, taught by nuns to speak the French French. My mother isn't as dumb as she seems to be. She can talk in a way that would surprise you, even a lively way, sometimes."

"She didn't speak the French French when I was there with her."

"No, she didn't."

"She hardly spoke to me."

"She's very shy, and you were strange to her."

"She asked me to make you happy."

"You make me happy."

Nancy kissed Yvon's chest and, because she liked to hear his voice as she fell into sleep, she said, "Tell me more."

"About my mother?"

"About anything."

"No, she's not dumb, my mother. She reads. Her favorite novel is *Maria Chapdelaine*."

"What is that?"

"A novel by Louis Hémon."

"I'm sorry, I've never heard of him."

"Well, it's a novel about us, or the way we used to be in Canada, a long time ago."

"A long time ago," she repeated.

And he repeated, "A long time ago."

Their talk seemed to her to drift, and all that mattered to her, and maybe to him, was the drift.

"Tell me about the novel."

"The doctor doesn't arrive to save the dying mother because of a snowstorm. Well, he wouldn't arrive in time to save her, not in a novel about us, no, in a novel about us the mother would die."

Nancy let her hearing go, then she brought it back. "Tell me more about the long history of the French you speak with your mother."

"You want to know?"

"I do, I want to know."

But he played with tangling and untangling her hair, as he would always do before he fell sleep.

She raised her head a little and insisted, "I do want to know."

He placed the back of a hand on his forehead, thinking, then said, "It's not interesting."

"It is to me."

He kept the back of his hand on his forehead to think of something interesting to tell her.

Nancy knew there was in him always too much to say, and so his long silences, but then, suddenly, he would become talkative, and then, just as suddenly, he would stop talking and say, "I can't," as if there were no words for him to continue.

He lowered his large hand onto her head and said, "Well," and she said, "Tell me," and she felt she was drifting off even more from what she asked him to tell her, what she wanted to hear from him, but there were no words for what he wanted to say, and none for what she wanted to hear. His hand moving in her hair, he said, "I can tell you there's a lot of history in the pronunciation," and she thought, what pronunciation? but she asked, "Oh?"

He said, "We don't say, in the French French way, 'moi et toi'; no, we say, 'moué pe' toué,' the way Le Roi Soleil" and he interrupted himself by raising his head from the pillow to ask, "You know who that was," and she said, "I know," and he lowered his head and continued, "Le Roi Soleil said, 'Moué je suis le Roué,'" and Yvon laughed a little and said, "It really doesn't matter," but, she tried to sound as though she meant it, "It does to me," and for a long while she felt his hand rounding out her head under her hair, and there came to her again the sense of something that couldn't be put into words, a sense she had never had with anyone but Yvon, with whom she was in bed, her head on his chest.

"And then," he said, "we say 'j'avions' instead of 'j'ai,' and that is what Molière uses when he wants his peasant to speak," and Yvon laughed more, embarrassed perhaps that he should make such a reference, but also that he should class himself among peasants. He immediately said, "The French colonists never used the word 'paysan,' no, they said, 'habitant,' because they left the word 'paysan' in France." He tugged at her hair and said, "So here we are in bed together, and you've learned a little about the long history of the French I speak with my mother."

"Tell me more about your mother," she said.

He said, "I can't."

She lifted her head so her long hair slowly pulled away from his chest and kissed him and said, "I've learned something I didn't know."

"There's so much to learn."

"Now close your eyes and we'll sleep," she said.

Which he did, and she thought, there is so much, there's too much.

Every Saturday morning, he left her for his parish, and as the weekend passed she felt more and more that he might not return. It was always a shock of relief to her to hear the doorbell on Sunday afternoon. Though he was now living with her, he would, as always, not presume to come in on her without first letting her know he was there. She ran down the stairs to meet him at the front door.

He sat on the edge of the bed, silent. Nancy stood over him.

She said, "It's been some time since you've told me a funny story about your parish."

He looked up at her and tried to smile.

Touching the tip of his nose, she said, "Tell me."

He took her hand in his, then leaned forward and pressed his nose and forehead into her stomach.

"If you don't have a funny story to tell me," she said, "tell me what the matter is with your mother."

Yvon raised his head then lowered it so it swung on his neck and said, evasively, "Oh."

"Come on, tell me."

He sighed. "Well, my mother wants to give in."

"Give in to what?"

"To what she wants more than anything in the world."

"What do you mean, Yvon?"

He said, "My mother wants to die."

This made Nancy draw back, in her feelings and thoughts as well as in her body. She lowered her eyes, then, raising them, she said, simply, "I've made a stew—I know you like stew—for dinner."

"Can we eat after?" he asked.

"After what?"

She became used to Yvon's impulses and was amused by them, as when, coming in from the cold so his red face appeared to be open with brightness that came more from within than without, he once said, his parka coat and gloves still on, "Let's go away."

As he took off his gloves, she asked, "Go away?" She unzipped his parka and opened it so it fell off his shoulders and down his arms.

"How much of America have you seen?" he asked her.

"A lot," she said.

"I haven't been anywheres," he said, and he corrected himself, "anywhere."

She hoped he would take a little joke that would make him think he amused her. "Anywheres?"

Now he assumed to correct her. "Anywhere."

She bit her lips so she wouldn't laugh. He did amuse her, he did.

He said, "I want to see, well, not the big things—you know, the Grand Canyon or the Old Faithful geyser or Yellowstone National Park—but the little things."

"What little things?"

"That'd be for us to discover, but the little junky things that most make up America, maybe, like motels off the highway, or hotdog stands on a beach, or a high school baseball game, or pitchers of beer and country music in a town hall, or a hand-clapping-and-swaying church service."

She shook her head, not wanting to say that he was being unoriginal. He believed he was being entirely original.

Yvon raised his arms wide. "Or just stopping in the middle of nowhere at night and getting out of the car to look up at the great big sky, the great big sky of America. Don't you want to do that?"

"I want to, but I won't. And neither will you."

He laughed and she, relieved, thought: now he was joking. Or maybe he wasn't, and she hoped he was.

"You're good for me," he said. "You're practical."

She suddenly said, "Not so practical that I'm with you."

"Does my being with you make you impractical?"

"Wildly impractical. Still, if I'm good for you, you're good for me," she said. "You make me want to do something wild."

"But," he said almost as if to mock her, "you know you won't, and I won't."

Her voice too high, she said, hugging him, "Let's go out to a club and dance."

He didn't hug her back, but said, "All right." She couldn't tell if he was agreeing just because she proposed dancing as a way of making up for hurting him, a way of doing something, or because he himself wanted to.

Whether or not he wanted to, in the strobe flashes from total darkness to momentary brilliance making him disappear and appear in different positions, he danced until sweat soaked his shirt. He danced as if in simply dancing he became possessed by a thrashing spirit. When he did appear in the flashes of light he seemed to be unaware of her, unaware of anyone; his ecstatic isolation awed her. If he couldn't go away geographically, he would go away spiritually, and he would go far. When, in a brilliant white flash she saw him, his head back and his eyes fixed on her, she imagined that he was not seeing her, but someone else. He closed his eyes and hurled his body about as if trying to break out of a narrow space. And she wanted him to break out and be the Yvon Gendreau who would possess her. Hardly moving, but raising and lowering her arms, her knees, modestly swinging her shoulders, she stared at him. She anticipated being back in the apartment, in bed together, his body still hot and wet with sweat, both of them possessed with the spirit of sex.

She had to sit, and she watched him.

As wild as he was, sometimes verging on violence, she was never frightened of him. In him there was no evil, evil having to do with intended violence; his almost-violence was always unintended. That was it: he was an innocent. Nancy, who was frightened of violence, allowed him the innocence of his violence. He was a wild boy from the forest, smelling of wood smoke, and in bed with him she allowed herself to lose her own control, as if she became a wild girl, as if, in making love, they were spirits dancing wildly together.

And if there was anything to give into, it was to give in to that spirit, though she knew that to give into that spirit was to fail in the world. Yvon was and would be a failure in the world, and would leave nothing behind for anyone to refer to, and everything he was and would be would be lost, as wild spirits were lost to the world, the only world there was, the only world to fail the spirits, the only world to fail the wild longings of the spirit, and Yvon knew, however much he would sacrifice this world for another, that there was no other, and that what he really longed for as he danced was to die.

Nancy had drunk too much, was more drunk than she had ever been. Yvon drove them back to the apartment, where she fell onto the bed, dressed, and sensed only his helping her undress and, under the covers, too, his naked body warm against hers, him holding her.

* * *

There was a thaw, and the ice melted in rivulets along the ground, the sun bright. And as if this revelation of the earth caused a revelation in Yvon, he came back early from his parish on a Sunday with what he called his rock-collecting kit in a canvas bag. He showed her its contents: a geological hammer with a blunt head and a pick behind the blunt head, two old chisels, one wide and the other point-ed, a magnifying hand glass, clear plastic containers with blank labels, a utility knife, a notepad and pencil, absorbent paper, gloves, and tools that, he explained, were used to ex-amine the rock specimens at home: bradawl, scraper, spat-ula, tweezers, dusting brushes, a bottle of diluted water, a pipette-topped vial of hydrochloric acid, and coins. If Nan-cy was only superficially interested in the explanation of all these—he used the coins to test the hardness of a stone—she was vividly attentive to Yvon's own elated interest. She suddenly saw dimensions in him she hadn't been aware of. The past gift of the quartz had seemed to her incidental, but to him, she now saw, it was essential—a dimension, maybe, of unexpected knowledge, of intelligence, of cul-ture. She was impressed, as though a child were suddenly articulate about the solar system and beyond—outer space as a subject that had nothing to do with him personally but that required impersonal study of worlds far beyond his, a sign of maturity.

To make up for having been too easy accepting his gift of the quartz, she asked him to tell her about its formation. As she listened to him say quartz was a mineral formed in rock at impossibly high temperatures at a time impossibly long past, and was made up of two atoms of oxygen and one of silicon, she was more aware of his earnest tone than of what he said, and she felt for him, for Yvon's attempt to engage in an outside world made up of mineral and rocks.

He said, "I thought, the day is so beautiful, we could go to the Blue Hills outside Boston and I'd show you a little about rock collecting."

"Of course," she said with tenderness, a slightly sad tenderness, which maybe underlay all her feelings for Yvon. But there was admiration, too.

She followed him along a path through woods to a stream below Great Blue Hill. "You know your way," she said.

"I come often. I get off the bus at the last stop it makes outside Boston, and it's only ten miles or so from there."

She watched him, with an ever-widening sense of his engagement—an ever-widening sense of tenderness, sadness, and admiration—as he, crouched by the stream, reached into the clear water and took out an irregular-shaped pebble, mottled rusty and gray-green, which he held in the palm of his hand to study. He placed it on a boulder and with the blunt head of the hammer tapped it. The sound of tapping appeared to make the surrounding woods go silent, as if invisible people there became silently attentive, and Nancy was in fact concerned that someone, a ranger, would emerge and arrest them both for Yvon doing something illegal in state park land, but Yvon seemed unconcerned, maybe assuming that he was in his interest outside even the law. The pebble fell apart into rough pieces, the largest of which he examined with his hand lens.

"What is it?" Nancy asked.

"I'm not sure."

She thought: he can't be so knowledgeable after all.

And yet he took notes, wrapped the piece in absorbent paper and placed it in a plastic container, and wrote the place and date on the label. Before he stood to leave with Nancy, he threw the other fragments of the shattered pebble into the river.

"Let's climb to the top of the hill for the view," he said.

"You won't do any more collecting?"

"That was enough."

Did he think she wasn't interested enough for him to continue, or did he feel embarrassed that he couldn't identify the rock, having set himself up as an authority?—maybe both, and she wouldn't press him because she was sure he would refuse all the more to continue. She wanted to tell him that, yes, she wasn't all that interested in rock collecting, but she was in him. He slung his canvas bag over his shoulder and again she followed him.

As they climbed the Great Blue Hill, there appeared outcroppings of blue rock emerging from melting snow, others from fallen leaves of the year before. Yvon had become silent in a way that made her feel she had caused the silence, though she knew that she hadn't, not really, that the silence was one with the shape of his character.

At the top of the hill was a tower of blue stone, its narrow door of thick planks, the heavy, rusted chain that was meant to lock it broken, and they climbed up. The view from the tower was of Boston, far off beyond pine trees bright in the late raking light.

She asked him, "Why are you so interested in rocks?"

He was terse. "You can't get more basic than rocks."

Back in the apartment, at the kitchen table he spread out the equipment for examining the rock more carefully, and Nancy, wanting to reassure him that she was interested, stood over him. He studied the fragment of pebble with his hand lens. She waited, wanting him to identify it, mentally urging him to know.

He looked up at her with an expression of amazement. "It's a meteorite."

"A meteorite?"

"My God," he said, "a meteorite. Do you know how rare it is to find a meteorite? So rare I never ever have thought I'd find one. And I threw most of it away."

He again studied the fragment with his hand lens, bringing it close to his eyes. He said, "It's a chondrite meteorite." Holding it up to her, he gave the lens to Nancy to study it. "Can you see the tiny embedded dots? Those are chondrules, granules of cosmic dust that floated around space from before there were suns and planets."

"Amazing," she said, trying to let him know she shared in his amazement.

He gave it to her and said, "It's yours."

She pressed it to her breasts and leaned over and kissed him, and he, now a boy growing into maturity, smiled at her appreciation.

"Maybe," she said, "I'll start collecting," and she stood it up against a wine bottle covered with dripped candle wax on the mantelpiece.

He was pleased, he was very pleased to show her something he knew that she did not know. Nancy told herself: she must remember, with tenderness and sadness and admiration, that Yvon was growing up.

In a continuing trance of awe, he repeated, "A meteorite, my God, a meteorite."

"If it is so rare," she said, "shouldn't you let some authority know?" and immediately she regretted the suggestion that he was not an authority.

He was contrite. "You're right, I'm not an authority. And I should let someone who is know. But I'm too ashamed."

Snow fell again when the Easter break came. She would go to New York to stay with her parents and he must go to Providence.

Again, Nancy said she would, on her way to New York, leave Yvon off in Providence. As she had more to pack than he did, he went into the kitchen to set the table for breakfast. From the front room, the Indian blanket drawn aside, she saw him holding a knife in one hand and a fork in the other, trying to decide which went on what side of the plate. He placed the fork on the right, the knife on the left, and she closed her suitcase on her bed and joined him. She thought he had to leave his world, had to, if not enter a world where knives and forks were assigned their set places next to plates, enter a world he didn't know, and he was ready.

Impulsively, she asked, "Why don't you come to New York with me?"

Having realized he'd got the knife and fork the wrong way round, he quickly exchanged them before he asked, "Come to New York?"

She laughed, asking, "Tell me the truth—have you ever been to New York?"

He, too, laughed. "No."

"Telephone your brother and tell him you're going to New York with a friend."

"He knows about you. He knows that we live together and that you're more than a friend."

"What does he think about that?"

"He's happy for me. And I know he'd be happy for me to go to New York with you."

"He won't mind taking care of your mother alone?"

"He's always telling me not to come on the weekends, always telling me to stay in Boston with you, always telling me that he'll take care of our mother."

"Call him now."

While he was on the telephone with Cyriac, Nancy listened to him speak the French she didn't understand, and she didn't understand it, she thought, because it wasn't anything like the French she had learned.

Hanging up the receiver, he said, "He said he's glad I'm getting away."

"And your mother?"

"He said my mother is glad too. My mother tells me, for my sake, that I should get away." He added, "This will be the first Easter I'll be away from her."

"Does that worry you?"

"I don't know. I go back, I go back to be with her every Sunday for Mass, because, you see, there's so little that keeps her alive, so little, and I try to give her some reason to go on living, and my going to Mass with her every Sunday gives her some small reason."

As they spoke, Nancy once again thought that she wasn't interested in Yvon's mother, and not really in his relationship with her, and yet she had never spoken so intimately with him about what must have mattered to him most.

Rain fell. The green interstate highway sign indicating the turnoff for Providence was dripping with rain. Yvon said, "Providence," then he went deeply silent as they passed all the turnoffs to his city.

Narrowing her eyes to see past the windshield wipers, she asked, "Do you really feel you can do something to help your mother?" and she thought that someone else, not she, had spoken.

"Oh," Yvon said, "no, not really."

"But you go."

"I go."

He didn't want to continue with the talk, and neither did she, but to show she was attentive to him, Nancy now asked, "What does your brother print?"

"He prints calling cards, leaflets for sales at the grocery, funeral cards, things like that for the parish."

He himself wasn't interested; eager to take in everything they passed, Yvon pointed out to Nancy, she didn't know why, a waterworks with water fountaining in round pools, an electrical power installation behind a chain-link fence, a cinder-block warehouse covered with spray-can graffiti. When they drove along the shore of Long Island Sound, he looked out at the gray water and gray sky. They stopped for a late lunch at a roadside restaurant, where Yvon kept rearranging the knives and forks on the plastic-topped table.

"I forgot to tell you," he said, "Cyriac asked me to give you his best regards."

"Thank him for me."

"And so did my mother."

"You mother did?"

"You heard her. My mother told you that she wants me to be happy."

Yvon insisted on paying the check and left too big a tip.

As if of themselves, lights of the city were beginning to switch on. Yvon, carrying their bags along the sidewalk of the side street, looked up to the right and left. A light went on in the window of a brownstone, revealing a woman wearing only panties.

Nancy said hi to the doorman of her building, and Yvon said hi to him also, his hi a little more friendly than hers. In the elevator he studied the wood paneling, the brass plate with brass buttons to press for the floors, and on the landing where they got off he studied the wallpaper patterned with fleurs-de-lys and a table with a vase below a mirror.

She opened the door of the apartment with her key and called out that she was home, but no one answered. Yvon followed her into the living room where a low-lit floor lamp with a big shade half illuminated the Biedermeier furniture, and she thought how strange this must all be for Yvon, who said nothing; she wanted it all to be strange to him and, with him here, she wanted it all to be strange to her, too. The floor-length curtains were drawn.

Nancy said, "No one's home."

She brought Yvon along the hallway into her room, where the bed, covered neatly with its white satin spread and many small white-satin-covered pillows, was made up as her bed in Boston was never made up.

Nancy said, "I'll show you where you'll be staying."

They went back along the hallway and into the dining room, where the wide dining table, holding a small but fully rigged silver galleon as a centerpiece, was surrounded by many chairs; a big painting of a platter of fruit above the buffet tipped out a little from the wall. Nancy pushed open a swinging door at the far side of the dining room and held it for Yvon.

She said, as they entered the kitchen, "I hope it's all right for you, staying in the maid's room. We don't have a guest room except for this."

"I don't mind anything," he said.

Off the kitchen, the maid's room was painted pale yellow and had a built-in wardrobe, also painted pale yellow. The narrow bed was covered with a pale yellow spread.

"But where's the maid?" Yvon asked, dropping his case.

"We don't have a live-in maid," Nancy answered. She put her arms around him and kissed him and whispered, "You'll come to my room after everyone else is asleep."

"Supposing they find out?"

"They'll make sure they don't find out," Nancy said, and she left him to go to her room with her case.

She found her mother in the living room, where, now, the

lights were brighter. Her mother was wearing a silk scarf loosely over her shoulders. When Nancy kissed her on the cheek, her mother said, "I just got back from the hairdresser," and with the red-nailed tips of her fingers she touched her bare nape. Her mother's hair was set in the smooth and even curves it was always set in. She said, "There's something I want to tell you, but I can't remember what."

"It'll come to you," Nancy aid.

Her mother asked, "Where's your friend?"

"Unpacking in the maid's room."

"How much did he bring with him that it's taking him so long to unpack?" Mrs. Green almost never smiled, so Nancy never knew if she was joking or not, and always presumed she was.

"I'll go see," Nancy said.

"Tell me a little more about him."

"You mean to ask, is he Jewish?"

"Please, you know me better than that."

"He's French."

"French, is he? Where is he from?"

"From Providence, Rhode Island."

"French from Providence, Rhode Island? What kind of Frenchman comes from Providence, Rhode Island? Does he speak French?"

"He does," Nancy said. "I guess I'd better go find out what's taking him so long."

"I hope he didn't come with black tie, expecting we'd be formal," her mother said. Again, Nancy wasn't sure if this was joking.

Yvon was sitting motionless on the maid's bed. She went

to the door and asked, quietly, "Do you want to stay here or come out and meet my mother?"

Yvon jumped up and said, "I've just been waiting."

"Waiting for what?"

"I thought it'd be more polite to wait for you to come for me."

"Why?"

"In case I met someone I hadn't been introduced to, wandering around looking for you."

"But all you'd have had to do was introduce yourself. They know you'll be staying. Come and speak with my mother."

As he followed her she thought, if he didn't impress her parents in any other way, he'd impress them with his politeness. He reached out a hand to Mrs. Green, who sat still for a moment to look at him, though she always seemed, in looking at someone or something, to be thinking about someone or something else. She said, "Nancy tells me you're French," and he answered yes he was. He stood where he was until she told him to sit. She was a tall, thin woman with pale skin and russet in her gray, molded hair. He sat in a chair angled to one side of the sofa, and Nancy, inserting both her hands under her own long, loose hair, shook her head and sat on the armchair to the other side. Yvon sat on the edge of his chair.

He said to Mrs. Green, "You have beautiful furniture."

She appeared to be thinking, not about the furniture or what Yvon had said about it, but about something that distracted her, and when she looked at Yvon, she said, flatly, "Oh, thank you."

"Really beautiful."

As if Yvon presented to her an opportunity to refer to something she assumed he knew nothing, or hardly anything, about, Nancy said to him, "Mom and Dad brought it all from Berlin."

But her mother said, "No. When we were able, we bought it all in New York."

Nancy, frowning, leaned forward. "You bought it all in New York?"

"When we were able."

"The ice buckets," Nancy asked, "you bought those in New York?"

"We did, yes."

Nancy sat back.

Yvon said, "It looks very expensive."

Mrs. Green smiled just enough for the corners of her lips to rise, and she said to Yvon, "Nancy says you speak French," but she seemed not to be entirely aware of what she was saying.

"Oui, je parle français," he said.

"And you speak French at home?"

"French and English."

Mrs. Green kept her eyes on Yvon; for once she actually seemed not to be distracted by something else. She said, "I would have kept up my French, naturally I should have kept up my French."

"I'll go get us some tea," Nancy said, and rose.

Her mother stopped her. "I know what I wanted to tell you. Gil and Maria have invited us for seder."

"Ma," Nancy said.

"I know, I know." Mrs. Green drew the corners of the silk scarf to cover her shoulders more closely. "Should I say we won't come?"

"I don't know, Ma," Nancy said again, and left.

Her mother called, "Nance," and Nancy reappeared in the double doorway, the wide white doors with round brass knobs open on either side of her. Her mother said, "There was something else." She thought. "But I've forgotten."

As Nancy left again, she heard Yvon ask her mother, "What's a seder?"

In the kitchen, preparing tea, it occurred to Nancy that she had wondered, at passing moments, how the furniture had been sent to New York from Berlin, because she hardly knew more than that her parents had left Berlin in a hurry. Maybe there was not much more to know. The question was: why did her parents want German-inspired furniture, why had they bought German porcelain ice buckets if Germany was a place they had to escape from?

She returned to the living room carrying a silver tray with a teapot and cups and saucers and a sugar bowl with tiny silver tongs and a milk pitcher and a dish of round slices of lemon and a silver tea strainer. Yvon got up quickly to take it from her and bring it, carefully, to the coffee table, as Mrs. Green told him to do. And as her mother poured out tea from a silver pot into a china cup, Nancy, with a little jolt, heard Yvon ask her, "And what else do you remember from Germany?" Not responding at first, Nancy's mother asked Yvon if he liked sugar and milk or lemon. He said milk and sugar, three lumps. Handing him the cup, she said to him, quietly, "What do I remember?" and Nancy, for the first time she could recall, heard her mother and someone her mother had just met talk about her childhood in Berlin. It wasn't that Nancy hadn't heard it before—her mother, sitting in the music room with her sister's beau, listening to her sister play notes that they had to try to identify—but she had never heard her mother talk about it in response to questions asked by a friend she had brought home, a friend from her mother had no idea where. When her mother said, "But you can't be interested," Yvon leaned forward and said, "But I am," and leaning further forward asked, "Did you ever walk under the linden trees in the spring?" Mrs. Green said, "Yes, we did, we did, I was a little girl, but I remember," and, untying the silk scarf and slipping it off her shoulders onto her lap and slowly folding it, said, "They were lovely."

Nancy was embarrassed that Yvon was asking her mother about a past her mother never spoke of to anyone not Jewish, and hardly to any Jew, and she wanted to get Yvon away. She suggested to him that they take a walk.

Before they left, Nancy's mother said to Yvon, "I hope you don't think we're very formal here. Nancy's father doesn't wear a tie to dinner."

"I told him," Nancy said.

Out on upper Fifth Avenue, Yvon kept looking across to the park, beyond the rough granite wall, its misty darkness lit in vague spots at distances from one another by greenish lamps.

"Can we walk in there?" he asked.

"I have never been in the park at night," Nancy said.

"Never?"

"Never."

"Let's go in now," he said.

She asked, incredulous, "You want to go into the park now, in the dangerous dark?"

"How dangerous is the dark?"

"We could get killed."

Laughing a little, Yvon said, "Come on, let's go in."

"You go."

"Not without you."

Hitting him on his shoulder, she too laughed a little and said, "Some other time, when we're good and ready to die. For now, let's get back to the apartment."

The apartment again seemed empty. Nancy said she'd have a bath and see Yvon in an hour in the living room, but, after an hour and a half, he wasn't there; she went to his room, where he was sitting on the edge of the bed, wearing a jacket and tie, waiting. She took him by the hand and led him out.

Her mother and father were in the living room.

As her father shook Yvon's hand, Nancy saw her father as a short, dark, bald man whose chin was so small it seemed to be one with his Adam's apple, and, yes, his hairy ears were big. He was wearing an open-collared shirt and a cardigan and slippers. His small hand fit into Yvon's big hand.

When they sat down at the dining table, a black woman came in from the kitchen with a platter of asparagus with silver tongs. Nancy introduced Hilda to Yvon, who, in too high a voice, said, "Hi, Hilda." She answered, in a low voice, "Hello, sir." Mr. Green took the asparagus with his fingers.

Nancy said to him, "Mom told me that Maria insists we go to her and Gil's for seder."

Maybe Nancy was imagining it, but she thought that Yvon couldn't decide whether to take the asparagus with his fingers or the tongs, and, after some deliberation, used the tongs.

Mr. Green said to Nancy, "And do we have to go?"

Mrs. Green sighed. "How can we not go?"

"We could use Yvon as an excuse," Mr. Green said and laughed a low laugh.

"I've never been to a seder," Yvon said.

In her nightgown, Nancy lay on her bed, the bedside light on, and saw by the clock under the lamp that a half hour had passed since she had told Yvon to come to her room. She went out and peered past his door, ajar, to see him sitting in a chair. He was wearing pajamas, a striped robe with a fancy twisted belt that ended with a tassel about his waist, and felt slippers. She had the curious sense that he was waiting, not for her, but for someone else. The sight of him wearing clothes she had never seen him wear, pajamas and a robe and slippers that he had no doubt thought he should have for his visit to New York, made her smile, and going to him her smile widened.

"What are you doing?" she asked.

"Waiting for you," he said.

She took him by the hand. Her room went totally dark when, in bed with him, she switched off her bedside lamp. He didn't move or speak.

"Put the light on," he said.

"Why?" she asked.

"I want to see you."

Reaching out in the dark, she touched the lamp and switched it on, and he, studying her face, lightly ran a finger over her chin, her nose, her cheeks, her forehead.

He said, "If I had been introduced to your mother as Irish, or Italian, or as Yankee, or, even more, if I were black, she'd have known exactly what to think of me. She has no idea what I am. I don't want anyone to know. I'm just an American."

To Nancy, the excitement of having sex with Yvon, though subdued, was that it was occurring in her home, in her room, in the bed she grew up in, where fantasies had originated and risen and risen and were now realized by the real body in her arms.

And perhaps the also-subdued excitement for Yvon was that he had never before made love in such a home, room, bed.

"Let's sleep now," she said, and he did what she told him to do.

She woke to her father calling her mother's name. Light showed round the dark blind over the window. Then she reached out and found that Yvon had gone.

She found him and her mother having breakfast in the kitchen; they went silent when she entered, and she asked, "What were you talking about?"

"Your mother was telling me more about Berlin."

Again, Nancy was astonished by her mother's willingness to reveal memories that normally she kept private.

As if realizing this herself, Mrs. Green said nervously that Gil and Maria had told her everyone should arrive before sunset, but Nancy insisted that for Maria sunset had never meant having to arrive before or after it, and she was not going to make an effort to comply.

She dutifully showed Yvon the sights of New York City for hours; she was glad that he didn't make many comments, and was even gladder when he said she must be tired and they should get back to the apartment. In the late afternoon she deliberately took her time getting ready, and when she and Yvon and her parents were in a taxi to Gil and Maria's apartment on West End Avenue, the sky was so darkly overcast it wouldn't have been possible to say the sun had set or not.

In the apartment, Nancy asked, "Where's Adam?" and Gil said, "He's in his room, and doesn't want to join us." Maria, her plump face bare of makeup and stark, said, "Well, it's his choice. I mean, I had a choice. He should have a choice. He likes to keep his beliefs to himself."

"So what are his beliefs now?" Nancy asked.

"As I said, he makes his own choice, but I've heard about the cult of people who wear dreadlocks and who in some ritual in Spanish Harlem sacrifice chickens."

Nancy said, "Sure," as a way of downgrading a conversation that she was uninterested in.

Gil, a slight man, wore a string of shiny blue beads on a leather thong around his open shirt collar. It hung down over his sweater.

Nancy said, "Gil, you're wearing your Hopi Indian beads."

"Yeah," he said.

The dining table, under a low-hanging, stained-glass Tiffany lamp, was set in a corner of the large living room. On it were a plate with three matzos, open bottles of wine, a glass tumbler of parsley, a bowl of salt water and a bowl of horseradish sauce, and four unlit candles forming the corners of a square within the circle of the round table. When everyone was seated, Maria handed out copies of instructions for conducting the seder.

Yvon, reading ahead, said, "Can I be the one to open the door when the time comes?"

Maria, not sure whether he was being serious or not, looked at him.

Mrs. Green said, "Of course you can."

"I know no man will want to read," Maria said. "It's wrong, it's very, very wrong. A man has to read. But as no man will, I guess I'll have to." She certainly did not ask Yvon to read, as if she knew by the sight of him that he was not Jewish. She would take over, and, as the leader, she began to read, but she didn't read the parts in Hebrew. She asked Gil to light the candles, and as he did, with a match, she read about kindling festive holy light.

Mr. Green said, "I remember a little of it in Hebrew: Baruch Atah Adonai . . ." He said to Mrs. Green from across the table, "You never learned."

She shrugged a shoulder, lightly,

"Will someone please pour wine?" Maria asked.

Mr. Green picked up a bottle and examined the label before pouring.

Maria said, "Now raise your glasses." Everyone did, and

she, holding hers in one hand and the instruction sheets in the other, half chanted, then she raised her glass higher, over her head, and read, "All drink the first cup of wine."

After a taste, Mr. Green winced a little.

Maria read more, then said, "Everyone take a sprig of parsley and dip it in the salt water." Everyone did. She said, "Now read where it says the group is supposed to read."

Yvon read louder than anyone else, even Maria, and because he did, Nancy, too, read out, but she wished Yvon would not try to take the lead, as if he was trying to show he belonged, Yvon Gendreau who didn't belong anywhere that Nancy knew of. He embarrassed her, so she looked at him with a little frown, which he saw, and did lower his voice.

"Eat the parsley now," Maria said.

Mrs. Green, who had been holding her dripping sprig between her thumb and forefinger, let it drop into her plate. She said to Yvon, "Go open the door."

"Great," Yvon said, and got up and went down the hallway off the living room and, narrowly in sight of the table, opened the door to the apartment.

Maria took a matzo from the plate and raised it just above her head, and she looked up to it, broke it in two, and held the two halves as she read from the set of papers lying on her place setting. Then she placed half of the matzo back on the plate; the other half she wrapped in a napkin and put aside.

Mrs. Green said to Yvon, "You can shut the door," and bowing his head slightly, he did and returned to his place at the table.

Maria read about this night of unleavened bread, and

the sense came over Nancy of being at a distance from the table. The more distanced the more the meaning of where she was expanded into a history too vast to be recalled to her in matzos, in a parsley dipped in salt water, in, especially, the bitter herb haroset. And yet, the more distanced the table the more meaningfully recalled in history were the parsley dipped in salt water, in the haroset, these bitter herbs meant to remind Jews of their suffering and now enacted in a ceremony that for a sudden moment she could not bear, and she closed her eyes.

"What's haroset?" Yvon asked.

"Horseradish," Maria said. She read the Haggadah, and at the end she said, "You can now drink your second glass of wine."

She broke the half matzo into smaller pieces and passed the pieces around and said to Yvon, "Break your piece of matzo in two, put some horseradish on one and cover it with the other, and eat it."

Yvon spooned a gob of horseradish sauce onto a piece of matzo, squeezed it down, so it dripped, with another piece, and bit into it. He shouted and pressed his hand across his sinuses.

Nancy saw her mother smiling lightly at him, and, maybe, a little pleased to think that he might be having some fun—her mother did like people who lightened her spirit. But Nancy knew that he wasn't, that, as a matter of fact, he was entirely serious in his enthusiasm.

Maria said to Yvon, "That is to remind us of the suffering of the Jews."

Yvon became still and closed his eyes, so that the others

at the table looked at him. Nancy studied Yvon, not knowing what he knew, but that he had to know, as all the world
had to know, of a suffering that she was removed from only
by her parents. Tears ran from his eyes down his cheeks,
and he opened his eyes and wiped away the tears with his
napkin.

He said, "The horseradish," and everyone except Maria
laughed.

"I'll go into the kitchen to bring out the roast lamb," she
said.

"Let me help you," Nancy offered.

In the kitchen, helping Maria transfer the leg of lamb
from the roasting pan to a platter, she heard Yvon ask Gil,
"Where did you get that necklace?"

Gil replied shyly, "A Hopi friend gave it to me."

As if she wanted to stay in the kitchen for a moment to
speak to Nancy, Maria said, "He's lovely but strange."

"Who? Yvon?"

"Where is he from?"

"From a village of log cabins in a forest."

Maria was not going to be taken in by Nancy, as Nancy
always tried to do, so she said, "Given how far out he is, I
suppose he would."

Picking up a bowl of hard-boiled eggs, Nancy preced-
ed Maria carrying the roasted leg of lamb. Nancy put the
eggs on the table, knowing that no one would eat them. She
saw Maria slip the half matzo she had wrapped in a napkin
from the table and hide it in the folds of her skirt as she
walked away, apparently looking for something. When she
returned to the table, she didn't have the wrapped matzo,
and was smiling. She said, "I've hidden the afikoman, and

now you've got to go search for it. Whoever finds it gets a reward."

"What's the afikoman?" Yvon asked.

Maria raised her eyebrows, but explained.

"Why did you hide it?"

She said, "Just so you can have fun looking for it."

"Great," Yvon said.

"Remember, someone has to eat a piece of it, or the seder can't be concluded. And nothing can be eaten after the afikoman."

But no one was willing to search for the afikoman except Yvon, and because he got up to start searching, Nancy, now wary of his enthusiasm, got up too, but only to stand by him and watch him.

"Don't go into Adam's room," Maria said. "The room with the door shut. He's in there and won't want to be disturbed."

"Maybe sacrificing a chicken," Nancy said.

"Oh, Nan, really."

Yvon, his enthusiasm raised to recklessness maybe by the wine, turned over the cushions of the sofa and armchairs, flipped up the corners of the rugs, took out books from a bookcase that held a small library on American Indian tribes—and didn't replace them. Mrs. Green smiled, and the others laughed, watching him, even, after a while, Maria.

When everyone laughed, he, sweating, smiled at them; this was what he wanted them to do, to laugh at him. Seeing him as though exposed in his lonely self, Nancy thought, And what is his history?

He found the afikoman under a newspaper on the coffee

table. After the clapping, to which he bowed, Maria went to him with a gift she told him to unwrap: an address book.

She said, "You must have a lot of friends."

Yvon kissed her on a cheek.

Mrs. Green said to him, "Eat some of the matzo, so Maria will let us go home."

That night he and Nancy didn't make love, but slept together. She was woken by him shaking her shoulder.

"Why did you wake me?" she asked.

He licked his dry lips. "Now I feel bad that I didn't stop in Providence to see my mother."

Easter morning he was so silent at breakfast that Mrs. Green asked him if he was not feeling well, which made him over-animated to reassure her that he was more than well. He talked too much, too loudly, about the great, really great, time he was having. Nancy's mother looked at her in a way to suggest that she do something with him that would really please him, as if she worried that up to now he had been pretending he was having a great time. Nancy, too, worried. What was wrong with him? she wondered. Her father was sensitive enough to apologize to him for not having thought he might want to go to church. Yvon laughed and said, "No, that doesn't matter here." But Mrs. Green knew that that was what was wrong: Yvon couldn't bring himself to say he wanted, on this most holy day for him, to go to church. She said to Nancy, "Why don't you take a walk down Fifth Avenue with Yvon?"

Silently understanding her mother's suggestion, Nancy took him down the avenue to Saint Patrick's Cathedral. Small groups of people were standing out on the sidewalk, and on the steps of the cathedral were two black women dressed, from high-heeled shoes to purses and small hats with veils, entirely in bright blue. Yvon stopped at the bottom of the steps, as if to stare at the two women; Nancy went ahead of him up the steps, but he didn't follow. She turned back to him and, seeing pain in his face, she went down to him.

"Let's go," he said.

At first she thought he didn't want to go in because, used to the primitive and stark church of his parish, he was intimidated by the cathedral.

"Please," he insisted, "let's go."

"I'm sorry," Nancy said, commiserating with him for something she didn't understand. She put a hand on his shoulder. "We'll go back uptown and take a walk in the park."

Like the boy he so often seemed to be, a boy who had been unjustly accused of a sin he didn't commit but was defenseless against, Yvon pressed the backs of both hands to his eyes, then, his eyes large with tears, looked away. Whatever he had been unjustly accused by, he was, she saw deeply, condemned by his darkness to accept, and her heart beat for him.

"Come on," she said.

It occurred to her to take him to the Museum of Natural History and, there, the gallery of minerals. His face brightening, he said, "What a great idea," still with a little sadness in his voice; when he repeated, "Really, what a great idea," she sensed that, in trying to reassure her he was also trying to reassure himself, because in his darkness no ideas were really great.

The dim gallery was like a circular space station, and around the walls were intensely illuminated vitrines looking backward out into the bright light of outer space, and the specimens of green, rose, purple, black, yellow, silvery, blue minerals, shining and shimmering, floated in that bright outer space.

Yvon walked past the exhibits and she followed, not sure if he was even glancing at the minerals. He walked more and more quickly; when they had made the circuit he stopped, facing the exit. She approached him slowly. His eyes were closed. She did what she had learned brought him, in some recognition of her affection, out of himself— she touched his cheek, and he opened his eyes and turned to her and smiled.

He said, "It's all too much"

Though she didn't understand, she said, "Then we'll leave."

As they walked around the park at the back of the museum, Yvon said, "The thing is I'll never know enough, never, never."

"Maybe you shouldn't want to know everything," she said.

And he, shaking his head, said, "Oh, but I want to know everything." She thought she wouldn't try to make him talk, would allow him his silence, but, as if he had thought this through and was now able to articulate the thought more fully than he had ever articulated anything to her, he said, "If you're a collector, you want every single example of whatever you collect—minerals, shells, stamps—so you become, well, you become possessed, and you have to make your collection complete. But you never can make it complete, because you want everything. Honestly, honestly, I don't know anything, and I should give it all up. I mean, give up everything." He raised a fist to his chest. "It's all too much, and I want to give it all up, everything, everything, that's what pulls at me." He dropped his hand.

"Yes," she said, and left the "yes" hanging in the air.

They were crossing a bridge, and he stopped to look down over the railing at a stream flowing among roughly jagged black rocks. Standing by him to look down, too, Nancy felt the pull, she felt it, but she didn't know, never knew, what the pull was to give in to.

She said, "Let's have a hot dog."

Yvon put an arm about her waist and pulled her to him.

Later, they met Vinnie in a café in Chelsea, its tables with little red votive candles on them. Yvon seemed never to have met anyone like Vinnie, and looked uncertain about whether or not he should like him. Vinnie told a joke about, he said, a queer who was so ugly he gave queers a bad name, but Yvon didn't laugh. His face was pale red in the light from the candle. His sexuality, Nancy thought, asserted itself and he was, yes, masculine in the way he crossed his arms and, silent, stared at Vinnie talking. Vinnie tried to assert his own sexuality with more jokes about queers.

To stop him, Nancy asked him, "Do you know anything about Aaron Cohen?"

"No."

"Nothing?"

"Nothing."

Uncrossing his arms, Yvon asked, "Who?"

"Someone I once knew," Nancy said.

"Who was he?"

"A Jew who converted to Catholicism."

"Why?"

"You're a Catholic. Maybe you could answer that question for me."

"No, I can't."

Before Nancy could speak, Vinnie said, "All I know about being a Catholic is that a Catholic has to abstain from sex." He showed his teeth when he smiled. "Do you, as a Catholic, abstain?"

"Stop it," Nancy said. "It's not funny anymore."

Vinnie pursed his lips and then said, "Well, I am sorry."

Yvon said, "I don't have any religion."

Alerted, Nancy asked, "You have the religion of your parish."

"Oh, the religion of my parish," he said, as if putting his parish at a distance from him. Nancy wondered if something had happened to him while he had been in New York to make him more seriously thoughtful than she'd known him to be, and, too, there seemed to be in his self-assertion a maturity she felt was new to her, if not to him. His voice was low, as if from the back of his throat, when he said, "That's lost in the forest."

Vinnie's voice rose. "The forest? What forest?"

Frowning, Yvon said, "The American forest."

Nancy reached out and delicately touched his deep

frown, and his forehead became smooth. He turned to her and smiled, but she saw an Yvon who might not last beyond New York, though, yes, maybe an Yvon who would last.

Vinnie said, "The American forest doesn't exist anymore."

As if Vinnie were not there, Yvon said to Nancy, "I think we should get back to the apartment," and the way he said "we" and the way he said "the apartment" made Nancy think, he has it in him, he does, to start a different life, and even if she were not going to be a part of that life, she felt enough for him that she wished him that different life. And maybe she could, maybe she did, love him.

As Yvon and Nancy were leaving the café, Vinnie said he'd stay on. He was short and frail, and when Yvon put a hand on Vinnie's shoulder and said, "Right on." Nancy thought he was not only condescending but using an expression that was pretended, because he seemed to have his own un-colloquial English. To try to make up for Yvon's assumed friendliness with Vinnie, Nancy embraced him closely, but he kept his arms by his sides, and when she released him he turned away. She wished she hadn't introduced the two men; she worried, a little, what Vinnie would say about her and Yvon as she watched him walk away.

Nancy's parents were in bed when she and Yvon returned. The light in the living room was dimmed, and Nancy, taking Yvon's hand when she turned off the light, guided him through the dark apartment into her room, where she shut the door and switched on a lamp beside her bed. He switched off the light when they were in bed together.

And if, she thought, she had once held Yvon in her arms with the sense of protecting him, he, now in bed with her, held her in his arms to protect her, or so she felt. Maybe she was wrong—it was always in Nancy to think she might be wrong—but maybe she was not wrong now, because she did feel his arms were strong around her.

This was their last night in New York. They would go back to Boston together, they would live together, eat together, sleep together, study together. But he drew away from her, and he didn't sleep.

She rose on an elbow and said, "You're thinking again."

"Am I?" he asked.

"Aren't you?"

"I guess I am."

"Tell me what you're thinking about."

"Oh," he said.

She lay back and said, "If it's about your not going to church with your mother on Easter Sunday, I'd say that you've gotten over that, or you've come a long way in getting over it."

He said, "Yes."

"You don't believe me?"

"I believe you."

"Then go to sleep. We should leave early tomorrow for Boston."

"I'll try to sleep," he said.

"Your thinking is keeping you awake?"

"I guess it is."

Nancy said, "When we were outside the cathedral, and

you didn't want to go in, I saw you had tears in your eyes. Why?"

He said, "I was wishing that my mother was dead."

Neither slept, and Yvon went to his room. Then Nancy slept fitfully, and when she went to Yvon's room she found him dressed. Mr. and Mrs. Green were out, but the breakfast table was set for them, with a note to wish them a safe journey back to Boston and Boston University, as if, Nancy thought, to emphasize education, with love.

On their way, when the first green interstate sign for Providence appeared, Yvon asked Nancy, suddenly, but as if in his long silence over the trip he had contemplated asking her, to leave him off at the train station.

She winced, but it did not surprise her, and she stated more than asked, "You want to go back to your mother."

"I do."

The abruptness of his wanting to be left off made her abrupt, too, even curt, and she said, "Fine," and took the exit for Providence.

She stopped at a curb before the train station and kept the engine running while he got out and took his case from the trunk. She knew that she shouldn't offer to take him to his parish, that he would refuse, but she didn't want him to have the choice of refusing; she refused for him by saying again, curtly, "Fine with me." He held open the car door on his side, now apparently unsure if he was doing the right thing, and he swung the door inward and outward a number of times in his uncertainty. He could open the door wide and get back into the car with her or shut the door. "Well?" she asked, and resentfully wanting him to shut, even slam, the door, she waited, wishing that he would get in. He shut the door and she drove off without saying goodbye, without looking back when she stopped for another car; she hoped she had impressed him with her resentment that he'd chosen not to stay with her but to go to his parish and his mother.

Then, unlocking the door to her apartment, she felt she had treated Yvon badly, that she had treated him badly because really she should have known that he had no choice. He had to go back to his mother.

She was not surprised at how lonely she was. At strange moments she felt that her loneliness was as deep as mourning for Yvon, who, now away from her, seemed to have died. She knew she felt these emotions—hurt as she was, angry as she was, forgiving as she was, lonely as she was—because she loved him.

She didn't see him all that week. Early on the following Sunday morning he telephoned from Providence.

"Have you been there all this time?" she asked.

He said that he had.

"But what about your classes?" She couldn't say, "What about me?"

He said, "I can't come back now."

And she felt she was giving too much of herself away, though she tried to keep her voice as if itself at a distance, "When will you come back?"

He didn't know.

Now she gave herself completely away. But he would come back, wouldn't he?

He didn't answer, and she thought that someone was listening to him speak, no doubt his mother. He said, "We'll be late for Mass," and he sadly said goodbye and hung up. Surely his mother had been listening, and surely his mother had allowed him to make the telephone call.

What hold did his mother have on him—his ailing mother with the dark Indian eyes who, Nancy thought, must have made him feel he betrayed her—for not caring for her enough, for not devoting himself to her needs, her demands. Of course she made him feel guilty for abandoning her on Easter and going to New York, even though Yvon had said that his mother wanted him to go, wanted him to be happy. And it came to Nancy: that Yvon's mother took it as a betrayal not only because he was away at Easter, the most holy of her holy days, but had spent Easter with a Jewish girlfriend.

She thought back over the Passover Yvon had so enthusiastically participated in—so much so that he may have been, oh, parodying being a Jew. Was that possible for him, who said he knew nothing about Jews? She had to put out of her mind that his mother probably objected to her because she was Jewish. She was in herself too aware of being Jewish.

Yvon suffered his mother, but she, Nancy, was not going to excuse him for his suffering. She would, in his absence, go to museums, to a concert, read books (she came, after all, from a cultured family; he had probably never been to the Fine Arts Museum or to Symphony Hall or read Henry James); she would see friends she hadn't seen since she had met Yvon, would see Manos. She was determined she would not miss Yvon; she would not wonder about him in his remote parish, with his mother and his brother, as if to wonder would be to be drawn into their primitive darkness.

Instead, she wandered about the small apartment, then lay on her bed.

Yvon's mother had wanted him to go to New York, had wanted him to be on his own, saved from her, saved from her kitchen and her house and her parish, from her religion, from her history, from her craziness, because she was crazy. But he still went back.

It seemed to Nancy that all of her thoughts were people, in a ring about her, and the people vied to stand out and stand steady and speak, and the one who stood out was Aaron Cohen, who said, "Yvon has his own longing."

She missed Yvon very much, missed him more than she had ever missed anyone else in all her life.

Next Sunday he didn't telephone, and she knew it was up to him to come to her.

Weeks passed and he neither returned to the apartment nor contacted her. And she told herself that—at least for now—she had to give up on him.

Awarded her master's in English, she stood in her cap and gown for photographs her father took. At lunch at the Ritz, where her parents were staying, her father asked her when she'd be getting back to New York, and her mother frowned at him for asking such a question, and frowned more when he, shrugging, said to his wife, "Well, I'd like to know what she's planning on doing." Nancy said, "I've got something I want to sort out here in Boston." "What's that?" her father asked, but her mother said to him, "Let her be."

Her parents walked with her through the Public Garden and the Common to her apartment. Entering before them, Nancy almost tripped on one of Yvon's shoes on the floor where it had been for several weeks; she tried to kick it under the bed, but, instead, it tumbled over into the room.

"How is Yvon?"

Her mother said, "Let Nan lead her own life."

But Nancy said to her father, "It's not a secret. Yvon's gone."

"Gone?" her father asked.

"Gone," Nancy repeated.

Her parents left Boston the next day.

As soon as they left Nancy tried to find Yvon's telephone number in Providence to call him, but he had never given it to her, and Providence information listed so many Gendreaus that she wasn't able to distinguish his. She had assumed only Yvon's family could have had that name. Then she thought that he would not want her to call him in his parish.

Irritated, she thought of going to New York, or, better, to Amagansett, leaving a note behind telling him, starkly, that it was up to him to get in touch with her on his return. But she was scared that he wouldn't return.

To distract herself she went out into springtime Boston to visit museums she had promised herself to visit. She tried to lose herself in shopping. She telephoned Manos and suggested that they meet, but he told her that he was dating somebody. He asked, "How are things with you and Yvon?" and she answered, "I'm waiting for him to come back from the dead."

On a warm afternoon, with an ocean wind blowing about her, she followed the Charles River across the wide, flat fens to the Museum of Fine Arts. The reeds along the riverbank shook in the wind. In the rotunda of the museum, at the top of a smooth flight of marble stairs, she stood for a long while before a painting, which, amid her preoccupations, appeared to go blank again and again.

She told herself she was not going to marry Yvon, was not going to live her life with him, have a family with him, become grandparents with him, and she was not because, primitive as he was, he was not someone she would or should marry. Because Yvon was a failure.

On her way back to her apartment she tried to make herself wish that he would never return, that she'd leave Boston and not ever think of him again.

But when she opened the door she saw him, naked, kneeling on the floor by the bed, swaying from side to side. She saw him just for a second before he was aware of her, and then he jumped up, turned quickly away, and ran to the narrow wall to the side of the big, curtain-less window.

"Yvon," she yelled.

His face contorted, he stood with his arms held out from his body, as if to expose himself in his nakedness totally to God.

"Why are you naked?" she asked.

He remained with his arms out.

Then Nancy heard herself say, in a high voice that was not hers, "Stop this." All at once hysterical, "Stop it, stop it," she cried.

He went to the bed and sat on the foot of it. His hands

hanging loosely between his knees, he hit them against each other, swung his head from side to side. He didn't look at her, hitting his hands together and swinging his head.

On the floor by the bed was a pile of clothes, and she saw a bloodstained shirt. She picked it up and held it out to him. Hardly moving her lips, she asked, "What is this blood? What happened?"

He continued to swing his head from side to side, in misery.

Nancy kicked at the clothes and saw that all of them were bloodstained, even the underpants, as if blood had soaked through to them, and she dropped the shirt onto the pile.

"Yvon, what happened?"

He shrieked, "The blood is hers. She did it. She did it."

Nancy stepped back from him and turned to look out the window, and with a flash of distraction she noted that the quartz Yvon had given to her was gone, and she didn't know what she had done with it, or the fragment of meteorite. She felt that she was alone, so the appearance of Yvon, standing before her was a shock. Rigid, she didn't react when he grabbed her. Her hair stuck to his sweaty shoulder, neck, cheek, fanned out in fine strands when he shook her. She tried to push him away with her elbows, shouting, "No," but he was stronger than she was.

And, after, his shoulder blades and spine jutting from his bare back, he turned away from her and lay down on the floor, motionless. She nervously combed out her tangled hair with her fingers. Without packing, without even washing, she left him, taking only her handbag, to go out to her car, where, her eyes closed, she shook violently, not weeping, but from time to time yawning in a way that made her shake all the more. She was still trembling when she turned the key in the ignition.

As she neared New York, trying to reassure herself that she was a woman of experience enough not to be broken by the violent actions of a crazy man, she promised herself, I will never see him again.

Her parents were not in New York, but in Amagansett. In the apartment, lying in her childhood bed, Nancy moaned, "Oh Yvon," and tears rose into her eyes.

three

The Greens' large, brown clapboard house in Amagansett was in woods, and Nancy, in the morning, went in her light nightgown and barefoot from her bedroom to the trees. The tall, thin trunks went up to high branches, where the early sun shone; she stood in the shadows below, among ferns. She walked among the ferns on dead, damp leaves. She saw the house, with its porch and wicker chairs, through the tree trunks. Her mother was at the screen door.

In the dining alcove, her mother poured out a glass of orange juice for her and said, "The Kenners are giving a party this evening."

"A party?"

"Don't you like parties anymore?"

"I guess I do," Nancy said.

Her mother put her hand on Nancy's head. "Are you all right?"

Laughing, Nancy said, "Why shouldn't I be all right?"

With her mother and father, she went into the Amagansett center for the Saturday shopping, and, as she had done as a little girl, stopped in the drugstore to buy her father a newspaper and look over the magazines in the rack; she chose two or three she once thought fun. With her parents she had lunch in a small restaurant, and in the afternoon they lay on chaises longues in the sunshine by their pool and, while her father read the newspaper and her mother dozed, Nancy flipped through the magazines, which were no longer fun. Lowering a magazine, she looked around, then looked at her parents, who, she knew, wanted both to protect her and to allow her all the freedom in the world, but Nancy felt no freedom was open to her.

The party at the Kenners was at dusk on a lawn behind their house. Kerosene torches burned, the flames wavering pale yellow against the pale gray sky, on stakes along the picket fence at the back of the lawn and down along the flagstone path to the pool. As Nancy, feeling her lightly sun-burnt body sensitive to the small, shifting movements of her dress, approached the people, she felt revive in her, just a little but enough for her to be aware of it, her old pleasure at going to a party. As soon as she got her drink, from a bartender in a white jacket behind a long table covered with a white cloth and bottles and glasses, she turned away from her parents to look around at who was at the party. One of the torches was smoking.

She saw a man standing alone under an apple tree near the house, his hands on his hips, looking around. He wore white flannel slacks, a white shirt, and a dark blue blazer, and his smooth black hair was combed back flat from his high forehead.

Nancy went to her old friend Eugenia Kenner, and, indicating the man in white flannels, she asked "Who's he?"

Eugenia said, "I don't know. But let's find out." She introduced herself as the Kenners' daughter, and he replied that his name was Tim.

"And this is Nancy," Eugenia said.

He was tall, with a large nose and a narrow face, his forehead high because his hair was receding. He appeared very neat, the collar of his starched shirt sharp-edged, and one button of his blazer buttoned. When he held Nancy's hand, he half-frowned, half-smiled. He was British.

Eugenia said she'd get him a drink, and, turning away to go, raised an eyebrow at Nancy.

She asked him what he did, and he said he was in law.

"A lawyer?"

"Oh, my ambitions are much greater than that."

Nancy noted how his tall body beneath his neat clothes appeared to be regularly exercised.

"Are they?" she asked.

As he was explaining to Nancy the difference between a solicitor and a barrister and a Q.C., Eugenia came back with the gin-and-tonic he had asked for, then, again raising an eyebrow at Nancy, left her to Tim. He was from London, in New York on a visit, and had been invited to the Kenner party by a mutual friend, Simona Morrow, who said she'd meet him here at the party, but he didn't see her, so he dared say he must have arrived before her.

Nancy said, "I went to London with my parents when I was a girl."

As if from a height, he asked, "And what do you remember?"

"I remember a soldier wearing a red uniform and a tall fur hat, standing at attention in the rain."

"One of the Queen's Foot Guards. Standing at attention in the rain is their duty."

Simona arrived, her hands raised palms out. Out of breath, she said, half to Tim and half to Nancy, that one of her children had suddenly become ill, but her husband had said he'd take care of him and insisted she come to the party to see Tim. Then she kissed Nancy on both cheeks and said, "Please excuse my agitation, Nancy dear. It's so lovely to see you again." She had become, Nancy thought, very British.

Simona and Tim began to talk about friends in London, and Nancy left them to find Eugenia. She said to her, "He sounds severe."

"Maybe that's just what we both need," Eugenia said.

As people were leaving the party, Nancy was standing silently with her parents when Tim came to her. She introduced him to her parents; hearing his name, Tim Arbib, Mr. Green asked him what sort of name Arbib was. He replied that it was a Jewish Egyptian name. Then Mrs. Green asked him what he did for amusement while he was visiting, and he said he liked to take long walks along the wide Long Island beaches. But before any more conversation could involve him, Simona called him away.

Sunday afternoon, while her parents visited friends whom Nancy found boring, she stayed at home. The sky was cloudy, the air moist. She became restless. She refused to think about Yvon. She telephoned Eugenia, but Eugenia had a date, and Nancy thought, we must grow up. When the idea of walking along the beach occurred to her, she realized it gave her a sense of possibility, one that had not come to her since she left Yvon, when all possibility had shut down on her. She drove to the ocean and walked where the surf spread out on the sand, among people walking their dogs. Beyond a long wall of boulders that Nancy climbed over, she saw Tim Arbib, his hands on his hips, looking out at the Atlantic. Though he might not have had any interest at all in meeting her, might have even been annoyed by it, she approached him, smiling so that when he turned to her he would find her smiling.

His reaction to seeing her was as matter-of-fact as though he had been waiting for her. "Join me for a walk?"

She swung her head so her hair swung. "Sure."

On a blanket among the low dunes of the beach were a man and woman in swimsuits. The man was kneeling over the woman, who lay on her stomach, and he was spreading lotion over her shoulders and back. Around them were pieces of driftwood, smooth roots of trees and broken planks, in puddles of water.

Nancy said, "I guess, after foggy, rainy England, the sun comes as a nice change."

Tim pursed his lips, then said, "That's not an altogether original view of England."

Anxious, Nancy said, "It rained all the while I was there, but I was there only a few days."

Tim said, "England is very often sunny."

"I guess I was there at the wrong time."

His eyes narrowed, he kept looking out at the ocean, and she thought he had lost interest in her because he thought her unoriginal. But he said, "Shall we sit on the beach?"

She followed him to where the sand rose into a dune grown over with dune grass. With apparently thought-out gestures he drew off his polo shirt with its little emblem embroidered near the shoulder. His chest muscles were narrow and taut and distinct, and his skin was matte white and his chest covered with curling, shiny black hair.

A young man, swinging his shirt and whistling, walked past them, and a vision of Yvon came to Nancy, a vision of him laughing and about to get into bed with her. And she thought: forget about him.

Tim sat on the sand, leaned back on his elbows, and looked again at the ocean, the tendons in his neck taut. Nancy sat beside him, her legs crossed like an Indian. Squinting, in the same way he had studied the horizon, he now studied her as he lay back and put his hands behind his head.

She looked away from his eyes to the blue sky, where the sun and the full moon both shone, the sun bright yellow and the moon pale white. Nancy didn't look back at Tim, but, aware of him staring at her, she said, "How strange."

"What's strange?"

"The moon and the sun out together."

His voice was a little hard. "What do you mean by 'strange?'"

Embarrassed, Nancy faced him and, laughing at herself, said, "I'm not sure what I mean."

"Are you an American mystic?"

"A what?"

"An American mystic."

"I don't know what that is."

"If you're an American you're a mystic."

"And what makes an American mystic?" Nancy asked.

Tim said, "To think that the moon and the sun out together must have some strange meaning."

"Well," Nancy said, "I'm American."

"So was my wife."

"Was?"

Then, very matter-of-factly, he said, "My wife is dead."

"I'm sorry."

He laughed a laugh from deep in his throat that might have been a cough. "Sorry for a thirty-year-old widower who doesn't really know how to run his life on his own?"

She wondered about this, but she laughed. "Yes, sorry for that."

"Thank you."

Nancy was wary of him but at the same time he roused in her some kind of amused, wicked spirit. She asked, "What strange things made your wife a mystic?"

"Everything had a strange meaning to her."

"Everything all together?"

"Everything all together."

Nancy lowered her eyes to take this in, then she raised her eyes to again see him staring at her.

She said, her voice high, "You're strange."

He said, "Look me straight in the eyes."

She did, and she saw that he was smiling a little, and she sensed her lips rise at the corners.

He said, "Don't look away, keep your eyes on mine."

She opened her eyes wide to fix on his.

He said, "I'm the least strange person you'll ever meet."

"Oh?"

"But I don't mind if you don't take me seriously. In fact, I would prefer if you didn't. I never like being taken seriously."

"Then I won't take you seriously."

"At Eton, we called this Eton bantering."

"Well then, teach me Eton bantering."

"You may be a good learner. My wife never learned. She was very serious."

"I'll try not to be."

"Do try."

"What did your wife die of?"

"Cancer—ovarian cancer."

"No children?"

"None. She couldn't. And I must confess, I would have divorced her but for the cancer. I'm not such a bastard that I would do that after she became ill. But I do want children. If I were to get married again that certainly would be a primary condition for marrying."

Nancy kept thinking: this was bantering.

"But supposing your second wife couldn't bear?" Nancy asked.

"I would have to divorce her and marry another."

"What about this—what about getting someone pregnant, then marrying her?"

"To be considered," he said lightly, "to be considered."

There was, she felt, a sophisticated lightness to their bantering.

Nancy said, "If you're alone and don't have anything else to do this evening, come have dinner with my parents and me."

Sitting up and putting on his shirt, he said, "It just occurs to me that if a middle-, or an upper-middle-, or, especially, an upper-class girl in England had said that, she would have put herself before her parents and said, 'Come and have dinner with me and my parents.'"

He was demonstrating his knowledge of the British class system, and if this was meant to impress Nancy, it did.

* * *

That night Nancy told herself it was the insects beating their wings against the screen that kept her awake. In her nightgown, she got out of bed and went to the window to look at the insects, their antennae vibrating as they danced on the mesh in fast circles around one another. She examined a large, motionless moth with soft dark wings, its pale eyes seeming to stare at her.

Back in bed, she couldn't sleep, and when, in the morning, still in her nightgown and bare feet, she went out onto the back lawn, a frightening longing rose up in her to see Yvon.

Her mother came out to her with a glass of orange juice.

"Will you be seeing Tim Arbib again?" she asked.

"I don't know," Nancy said, and then, not to disappoint her mother, she added, "Probably."

"I'll invite him again to dinner if you want me to."

Tears welled up in Nancy's eyes, and when she blinked the tears ran down the sides of her nose. "I think I should go to Boston for a few days," she said, "just a few days."

"I understand," her mother said.

"Has Dad already gone back to Manhattan?"

"Yes."

"I'll leave after breakfast."

Nancy walked across the lawn to a lilac bush. She broke off a branch of lilac, and, the bush shaking, a mass of insects flew out and around her. The sprig of lilac in her hand, she stopped, or felt she was stopped, in the middle of the lawn, by the overwhelming feeling, occurring like a dark, arresting circle around her, of her deepening longing for

Yvon. Looking at the sprig of lilac in a hand that wasn't her hand, she felt that someone else, not herself, was standing where she was, longing for what she herself could never want, could never long for. The sprig of lilac appeared stranger than any plant she had ever seen before, the insects flying around her appeared stranger than any creatures she had ever seen before; the house and the woods appeared to her the strangest place she had ever seen before. There could be no stranger world than the world she stood in, if it was she who was standing in it.

She thought she would get out of that world, too strange to her, and live in a familiar world, even if this world were not very happy. And she would do this by going to Boston and seeing Yvon for the last time.

On the highway to Boston, a low-slung car with big tail fins passed her, the windows open. In the front seat were two young guys, bopping their heads to loud music. Two large soft dice were dangling in the rear window. They appeared to be so happy. She arrived in Boston as the sun was setting.

She had her keys to the street door and to the apartment on Beacon Hill, but, as Yvon had done when they were living together, she rang the bell at the street door instead of going in and surprising him. He didn't appear. She opened the black door, climbed the bare wooden stairs to the landing, and stood for a moment at the door to her apartment, as if waiting for him to open, before she opened it herself.

Entering the hot apartment, the windows all shut, she startled Yvon, who, lying on the bed in his underpants, jumped up on seeing her and stood as if at attention. The unmade bed smelled of his body in the sun-filled room. As she stared at him, he slowly raised his arms and, as if to protect himself, crossed them over his bare chest and grabbed his own shoulders.

"I'm sorry, I thought someone made a mistake ringing the bell."

She said, flatly, "I came up to Boston to get something."

With the same flatness, he asked, "Oh?"

She had no idea what to tell him she had come for.

He asked, "Would you like some cold tea?"

"I would like some, yes."

From the floor he picked up a pair of chinos, which he drew on, then he took a shirt from where it hung on the back of a chair and put it on and buttoned it.

"I was just resting before I go off to teach," he said.

"You teach?"

"I got a job teaching French in a language school."

"Then you've found a practical way of using your French."

"I'm trying to be practical."

He held out a hand for her to go ahead of him into the kitchen, where they sat at the table with tea in tall, thin glasses with patterns of flowers on them. She tried to center her thoughts and feelings away from him, on the rim of her glass, but she was drawn, and all her thoughts and feelings with her, to his lips, his jaw, the hollow at the base of his throat. She looked at him closely, at the lobes of his ears, his eyebrows, his sweat-moist forehead.

What did he think? Did he think that his mother killed

herself because he went to New York and not to her in the parish? Whatever he thought, his dead mother now denied Nancy and Yvon any possibility together.

Rising, Yvon said, "I'll leave you on your own to get what you came for."

"You don't have to do that."

He remained standing at the other side of the table. "I should be going to school for my evening class."

She knew in all her body that if she didn't let him go now, she would do something to make him stay, though she had no idea what that could be. As strong as it was, it couldn't be more than the desire to lie on the same bed with him, in those sheets saturated with his smell, couldn't be more than the desire to lie next to him and fall asleep with him. Nothing more than that? She was very tired, more tired than she could stand, and at the same time she felt, in all her tiredness, a tightening of her muscles and tendons that made her hold out her hands, her fingers curled, to grab something, to grab him, across the small table and, knocking over the glasses of tea, pull him towards her and, oh yes, bite his lips, knock over the table by pulling at his shirt so he stumbled after her into the bedroom and onto the bed. No, no, not that, not that; but something more than that, something that sex could never realize; something that had to be fought for through flesh and bone if it was to be had at all. He knew what this something was, he knew it more than she did, more than she ever would, and she must have it in repossessing him. She felt, as she had never before in her life felt, a rush of passion for that something he embodied in his arms and shoulders, in his chest and thighs and legs, in his very smell, which she must have, which she would have.

But she sat still, and, though her feelings made little spasms pass through her, she held herself back from giving in to the impulse to reach out for him as she watched him, standing above her, place his hands on his cheeks and close his eyes.

He opened his eyes and said, "I need to go to school."

She stood. "Let me lie on the bed next to you," she said, "just that. I won't touch you. I'll lie next to you. That's what I came for. That's everything I came for."

Yvon kept his hands to his face.

"Do I have to beg?" she asked.

He dropped his hands and turned away.

She sank cross-legged on the floor next to the chair, and, her shoulders slumped and her hands in her lap, she sobbed, but Yvon didn't come to her.

Her whole body aching, she got up long after she heard the door to the apartment shut.

Before she left, she looked for the quartz and the fragment of meteorite, wanting to take them away with her, but they were gone.

At sunset, wide and gray-purple, cars along the highway switched on their lights, and as the dark deepened, the white and red lights flashing past her were all she saw. She was so tired that, after a moment of abstraction when the lights of the traffic appeared to drift up and away as though the cars were turning off in an unexpected direction, she left the highway to get a cup of coffee.

Twice more she stopped for coffee. She imagined that off

the highway, in the nighttime woods, people were standing, illuminated by beaming car lights. She was still closer to Boston than to New York. She was sweating, and she felt that her clothes were dirty and twisted about her, that her hair was dirty.

Halfway to New York she stopped again, this time to eat. The restaurant was crowded, and she, at a small table next to the large table of a family with a baby in a highchair, couldn't eat the food she ordered. Her head began to throb. She paid the bill. Outside, the cars in the parking lot glared in the floodlights. For a while she couldn't find her car.

The expressions on Nancy's mother's face appeared to have been slowly thought out, and, with simplicity, she put a hand on Nancy's arm and told her that Tim Arbib had left a message.

Nancy had never imagined that she, a free spirit, could be so emotionally and bodily constrained, with no sense of possibility. Standing long under a cool shower, cupping the water in her hands as it fell and splashing it against her face and body, she thought perhaps she understood the need for purification. She let the water pour over her head, down though her long hair that, dripping, flowed along her body as though her hair too were water, and her skin water.

Because she thought meeting Tim Arbib might confuse her, she waited some days. She dressed in a loose gray pull-over, a gray skirt, and black pumps, her hair simply brushed back from her face, the simplicity meant not so much to protect her as to make her appear serious, because she was serious, and if he had any appreciation of her it had to be that she was serious, and that with her he was, too—not the bantering girl he had met, but a woman whom he must treat as a woman, a serious woman. If he did not respect her as she insisted on being respected, she would make every effort to protect herself against him; then, back in her room and on her bed, she would lie, a broken girl.

She held out a hand to him to shake, but instead of grasping her hand, he lightly pressed the tips of his fingers against hers and turned her hand as though to raise it and kiss it, a gesture she felt would be both formal and intimate, and respectful. But he didn't kiss her hand. She smiled a smile that lifted only the corners of her mouth. It seemed to her a smile that made her invulnerable.

Though she knew the Hamptons better than he did, she felt directionless, and let him lead her. Five minutes into the date she found herself wishing she were in her room, lying on her bed in a dim room, the blinds drawn against the sunlight.

The restaurant, chosen by him, was in a large, white clapboard house with a massive fieldstone fireplace, their table at a window with a view of the sunlight on the ocean.

He said, "I do like a view."

She hadn't before noted the view as special, though she'd been to the restaurant often with her parents. She realized she had hardly spoken, leaving talk up to him and she responded briefly, distracted, but not able to say what distracted her. She must make an effort.

"Do you go to places for the views?"

As if incidentally, he said, "My wife liked views. When

she was ill, I made a point of taking her to places she particularly liked for the views. We went to Scotland, to the Highlands, because she had a great desire to see the stark mountains. That was the last. Afterwards, she wasn't capable of travel."

"A longing to see the stark mountains."

"A great desire. That's what she said. I didn't, and don't, understand, but I sat with her on a bench outside the modest bed-and-breakfast where we were staying, about ten miles from the house of some good friends of mine, and I wondered what her great desire was in looking at the mountains ranging before us. I remember there was a deep valley between the mountains, and rivers and waterfalls in the valley."

"And you were never able to understand her longing?"

"Longing? No, not longing, that's a word I would never use. It was all I could do not to make a joke of her desire for views. She knew I wouldn't understand, knew, I'm sure, that I would deride her, gently, I suppose, but deride her for her pretensions for such views."

Nancy asked, "Pretensions?"

And he said, "Let's order," and they did, and as if he had intended to continue what he had been saying because it was important that she understand him, this elegant man from, maybe, Egypt, said, "I actually think she relied on me for my derision. I knew she didn't want me to take her soulful longings seriously. I might say to her, when she withdrew as if alone with her vision, 'Darling, let's just have sex,' and she'd laugh."

"And did you then have sex?"

"Often."

"You weren't deriding her, I think, but teasing her."

"No, I was deriding her."

Nancy thought: he is warning me.

Surprising Nancy, Tim said, "Miriam is dead, and I am alive, and that is everything."

"Everything," Nancy said.

"You understand."

"I think I understand."

"Well, then I can tell you I feel that though I couldn't have saved her against death, I should have, somehow. But I didn't save her."

"And you blame yourself for that?"

"I do."

Nancy leaned towards him. "And that's grief."

"You know grief?"

"In a way, I do, yes." She paused. "Yes, I do."

"For someone dead?"

"Someone I was once involved with. I never understood him. He frightened me."

"He threatened you?"

"I suppose he did."

"If I had been there—"

"Thanks, but I think, in the end, he was more threatened than I was." She spread her fingers out on the edge of the table. "In a way, it's as though he were dead. He's the one I grieve for. What you feel about your wife, your feeling you could have saved her though you knew you couldn't, that's what I feel toward him—that I could have saved him, though I knew I couldn't have."

"You stopped seeing him."

"Yes."

"Is your will strong enough?"

"You mean, against my will, will I see him again? I mustn't, but I do need a strong will."

"How?"

He was attentive to her with a slight—a slightly seductive—smile. She smiled too. "You tell me how."

"Learning Greek? Learning to play the violin? Learning symbolic logic? They all require willing oneself to learn." Now he laughed, and she thought, with surprise: I am actually enjoying this. He said, "Learning all the forms of law?"

They sat back from the table for a waiter to serve them. She asked, "Will you tell me more about your wife?"

"Anything you want to know."

"She was Jewish?"

"Of course."

"Where from?"

"Texas."

"How Jewish was she?"

"Only in that she, from a rich Texan Jewish family, would have married a Jew, no more than that."

"And you?"

"I would only marry a Jew. And yet I don't go to temple. I go more often to Anglican services for weddings, baptisms, funerals, memorials. One can't grow up in England without participating, over and over and over, in Anglican services. I sing out the hymns with the best of them, sing them out with more conviction than an Anglican, none of whom I know actually believes any more than I do. The hymns are simple, so simple and so transparent, and in their simplicity and transparency very beautiful."

"Very beautiful."

"Well, if you were to come to London, I'd have you singing full voice in church."

"I'd like that."

Then he said, with simplicity and earnestness, "I have to admit I am not a deeply feeling person, but I am honest and open and have no secret desires."

And for the simplicity and earnestness of his words, Nancy thought she could rely on this man for his honesty, his openness, his having no secret desires. And she knew that he was confessing to her for her understanding, what he would never confess to anyone else. And this occurred to her: he was proposing to her.

As they talked, the light on the ocean lengthened until it appeared to be, itself, an ocean of light.

Tim's lovemaking was intentional, methodical, and this was all right with her. She had had lovemaking that was out of control, and she was reassured by his control. With careful deliberation, he made sure she was as satisfied as he was. And, after making love, he surprised her by saying, "Thank you."

He flew back and forth from London to New York to see her and they always stayed in a modest but good hotel. Mr. and Mrs. Green liked Tim, or they told Nancy they did, but she knew they would never invite him to stay with them, as if they considered her relationship with Tim a relationship apart, Tim more than a boyfriend to their daughter, whose independence they had always respected. When she told Tim she was pregnant, he proposed marriage in a very straightforward way, starting with, "Well now——." She accepted, but she soon realized that to be straightforward was what she too had to be.

This seemed to be his principle: whatever there was in his life that he did not explain needn't be explained, because it was obvious, and the obvious explained itself. He explained the practicalities she had not quite considered, and he took care of the practicalities.

Nancy wondered if her entire relationship with Yvon had been based on pretension, on the pretentious attraction to, oh, the strange. Tim would have made her aware of that pretension. She wanted now, if not the familiar——for Tim's world was not familiar to her——the simple, even though rigorously defined. She needed rigor.

Tim wanted the wedding, in New York, to be simple. His parents came from London, and an old friend from Oxford days to be best man. After the wedding Tim returned to London with his parents to prepare, he said, for Nancy, and she, now a married woman, continued to live with her parents as if she were single. She took notes on an article she thought of writing about Henry James.

As Nancy walked around the reservoir in Central Park, she thought about Henry James, and she wondered how she could expand on the so-often-repeated word "everything" in his novels: how so often the consequences of a dramatic con-

versation rose to a level where one of the characters said, "everything," though the summation of "everything" was never
explained, yet, as James so often wrote, "hung together."

And, she wondered, what could the word "everything"
mean, because, in fact, the word only existed in itself?
There was no having "everything" unless you had every
single thing in the world. Still, within the world of Henry
James, "everything" did "hang together."

As she entered the living room of her parents' apartment, she saw them standing by the fireplace, he with a
sheet of paper in his hands, a letter, Nancy supposed, because an envelope lay on a rug on the floor. Usually when
she came into a room her parents were in, they immediately turned to her and smiled, and often enough her father
held out his arms to her for a quick hug, but now they were
both concentrating on the paper her father held, and as she
approached she saw her mother's eyes magnified with tears.
Alarmed, Nancy asked, "What's the matter?" but her mother simply looked at her. Her father, with a deep frown, folded the piece of paper and Nancy reached down to the rug
for the envelope to hand it to him. He slipped the paper into
the envelope, closed the flap, and said, as a fact, "After all,
the search has been abandoned," and he put the envelope
into the side pocket of his jacket. In a low voice he said,
"We'll go have dinner now." Nancy's mother, her hands to
her cheeks, followed him into the dining room. Her father,
at the doorway, called Nancy to come, in a low voice.

At the table, Nancy noted that her mother's eyes were
red. Hilda came in with a tureen of soup and placed it on
the table, and Nancy's mother served the soup.

She asked Nancy, "Do you ever hear from that Yvon?"

"I don't, no."

"I suppose he was strange."

"Yes, he was strange."

"But I liked him," Nancy's mother said.

"I did too, I liked him, but he was not for me."

Her father asked, "And you're sure Tim is for you?"

"I'm not really sure of anything, Dad, but I think I have a better chance of getting along with a Jewish man."

"That's for you to see."

Nancy repeated, "That's for me to see."

She thought how everything that was said seemed to sound within a vast empty hall.

Hilda cleared away the soup plates and served the main course.

Nancy asked, "What search was abandoned?"

Her mother answered, "For my mother."

Her father said, "It was no surprise, because we waited so many years to learn what we already knew."

Nancy tried to keep her voice in accord with the silence of the vast, empty hall. "And you don't know in what way she died?"

"We tried, we tried," Nancy's father said. "And maybe, after all, it's better that we don't know. The search is abandoned."

"How can you bear not knowing how she died?" Nancy asked them.

Nancy's mother answered, "We bear it because we have no choice."

After the silent dinner, Nancy, sitting up in bed, tried to

read, but she couldn't, and often dropped the book to her lap and stared out.

"Everything," she said, just the word, "everything."

When she knew her parents were in their bedroom for the night, she went to them. Her father was in the bathroom, her mother lying in bed; Nancy lay down next to her and her mother drew her close and Nancy rested her forehead against her shoulder. In his pajamas, her father came from the bathroom and sat on his side of the bed. Nancy moved to get up, but he said, "Stay with us," and she lay with her head on his pillow, and he lay by her, and by his breathing she knew when he had fallen asleep.

"You should go back to your bed," Nancy's mother said.

"Let me lie here a little longer," she asked.

"A little."

But her mother reached out to the lamp by her side and switched it off, and Nancy fell asleep with her parents.

In the taxi into London from the airport, Tim looked out of the window at his side and Nancy had the sense that whatever he was thinking about, it was not her.

Finally she asked, "Are you thinking deep thoughts?"

He turned to her slowly. "Deep thoughts? What rubbish," he said playfully.

And yet she found herself apologizing.

"I was thinking about the champagne, ready for us in the fridge to celebrate."

She laughed and put a hand under his elbow and leaned closer to him. "That's thinking deep enough for me."

He placed an arm across her shoulders and kissed her temple.

Maybe, she thought, he was teasing her.

She expected Tim's house to have a wide white façade, front steps leading up to a wide black door, with, of course, a brass knocker, and on either side of the door, maybe, pilasters holding up a pediment. The front garden would have grass and, in tubs, shrubs on either side of the steps. There would be an iron gate in a white wall along the pavement and a gravel path to the steps. And the inside shutters of the wide, many-paned windows would be closed, or half closed; she would open them. She expected simplicity and spaciousness, bare, shining parquet floors, and a large mirror above the marble fireplace. She saw what she imagined to be such houses from the taxi.

On a side street in Hampstead the taxi stopped in front of a narrow brick house with narrow windows and a high, stepped gable. An iron scroll-work gate in a low brick wall opened onto a brick pathway and a red front door. Gravel covered what couldn't be called a front garden. Tim carried his briefcase, followed by the taxi driver, Nancy behind the driver. The driver deposited their two suitcases on the brown-tiled stoop, was paid, and left. Around the red front door were little multicolored glass panes.

Nancy realized that she had known, without having to be told, that Tim could not have afforded the house she had imagined, and that he, who would never apologize, had not described the house because describing it might have sounded like an apology. He would not apologize for himself.

He held the door open for her and she walked down a

narrow hall, a stairway at the end, and as she went along paintings on both sides of the hall appeared and disappeared, small paintings in heavy gilt frames: camels and an oasis of palm trees, a veiled woman sitting on a cushion, a pyramid against a sunset.

She turned to Tim, who, having brought the cases inside, was closing the door. She had never before heard herself sound so affected. "What are these lovely paintings?"

"Nothing more, really, than picture postcards."

"Where do they come from?"

"They're a collection I've been putting together."

He was being elusive, and so, too, would she be. "Oh."

He opened double doors, dark and paneled, into the living room, and stood aside for her to enter, and she saw, in a blur, not simplicity and spaciousness, but unexpected complexity and clutter. This couldn't be Tim's living room, not the Tim she was married to, the Tim she thought she knew for his personal sense of order. There emerged from the blur a leather Chesterfield sofa and leather armchairs, the kind she imagined were in men's clubs, and paintings—camels striding across a desert, a moon shining on an oasis, three pyramids of diminishing sizes in a sunset. How odd his taste in art was. Nancy walked slowly around the room and noticed tiered shelves on which were displayed brass water jugs, rows of ancient terracotta oil lamps, small clay or faïence statuettes, dull glass vials, fragments of marble. On the floor was a large Oriental rug, the pile silky, and on a large round embossed copper tray supported by a stand were ceramic bowls patterned in blue and green; hanging over the edge of one was a strand of Muslim prayer beads in red amber with a red tassel. A Scottish plaid throw rug, folded neatly, lay on the seat of one armchair and before the armchair a pouf upholstered with an old embroidery on canvas, a long fringe hanging round the bottom edge.

Tim stood in the middle of the room.

"You collected all of this?" Nancy asked.

"I suppose it's my way of trying to reproduce the world of my parents in Alexandria before they left."

"Why did they leave?"

He frowned. "You don't know?"

She tried to dispel his frown by saying lightly, "I'm afraid I don't."

He frowned more. "All Jews were expelled from Egypt."

"Why?"

Tim was, she saw, disappointed, and she felt that she had revealed something about herself she shouldn't have, revealed that she was a stupid American who didn't know history, or so he would think. "Don't bother your head about that."

"But I want to know."

"Leave it."

"I won't leave it. I want to know."

His face tensed. "We arrived in London, refugees, and that's enough to say. You needn't know more."

And she did know him well enough to leave it. For a flash, she wondered if he was putting her in the place where he wanted her to be, and where she would accept being. She didn't have to know. She pointed to a room beyond the living room, to which double doors were wide open. "What's in there?"

"My study."

Still dazed, she went in. Books lined the walls, even on either side of the chimney breast, where there was an elaborate fireplace and, over the mantel, a framed page of Arabic script, black on gold.

She thought she wouldn't ask what the script meant, but, singling it out by gazing at it, let him assume she had her own appreciation. She said, "Really lovely."

"Thank you."

She pointed to a table in the center of the room piled with books, and among the books, standing upright, a gleaming silver case embossed with swirls surrounding small tablets with Hebrew letters in gold and topped with what looked like a delicate crown, within it tiny gold bells. To either side of the crown slender silver posts supported elaborate globes from which hung, all round, more tiny gold bells. Wanting him to know she was not entirely stupid about Jewish matters, she said, "I've never seen a Torah cover like this one."

"Sephardi. You would be used to Ashkenazi covers."

She would be as stupid as he wanted her to be about everything, but at the same time she would try to make him think she wanted to know everything he had to teach her, if he wanted to.

"Where is it from?"

"It belonged to my great-grandfather, who was chief rabbi in Aleppo, Syria."

"It's too much for me to take in right away, but I will—I shall—take it in, all of it. It's all so great."

Nancy thought to herself: make the world as real as real as can be. Then she felt like a fake for thinking this. Holding Tim close to her, she pressed her pelvis against his, but as she did she thought: I'm acting.

She drew away and jerked her shoulders as if dismissing everything, real or unreal, and said, "What about that champagne?"

"Go upstairs and look around and make yourself at home. Our room is the one overlooking the back garden. I'll bring the champagne up to our room and find you already bathed and in bed."

"Resting?" she asked.

"No," he said, "not resting, but wide awake." And to Nancy this sounded vulgar.

She said, "I'll be waiting."

And she lay waiting, as he had asked, in an unfamiliar bed in an unfamiliar bedroom that was not to her liking.

She heard him in the bathroom splash in the bathtub, and heard him sing as he dried himself, and heard a cork pop; and she sat up when, naked, he came into the bedroom, two flutes crisscrossed at their stems in one hand and the open bottle of champagne in the other.

He climaxed, shouting, "Fuck!"

Why did this shock her? It shouldn't have. He was frank about sex, as he was frank about everything. She wanted to like this frankness. He rolled off her and said, as he always did, "Thank you, darling, for that."

She sat up and, looking about at the room, said, "I'm going to redecorate this room."

"You can have this room," he said, "but not the sitting room or my study. You won't touch those rooms. Promise?"

She promised.

The next morning she woke alone and saw that rain was falling in the garden, and she went to the window to see the rain so heavy on the roses that the petals opened and dripped, and she felt very alone. In her robe she wandered about downstairs, thinking, this is my home now, but at the double doors to Tim's study she hesitated, listened, then quietly opened the door.

She saw first the Torah in the middle of the room, and then, beyond, Tim at his desk, and she stepped back. Leaning forward, he said, "Nancy, Nancy, come in," and he smiled.

"I suppose I was curious," she said.

He rose from his desk to go put an arm about her and draw her to him, and she leaned against him.

She said, "I watched the rain fall in the garden, making the roses so wet that the petals opened and dripped."

"Beautiful," he said.

"You like beautiful things?"

"I do, yes, I do," he said, and kissed her temple. "Come sit with me on the sofa."

She did as he asked, and there he covered her with another Scottish plaid, which appeared to come from a country that had nothing to do with the house.

As though he'd held off until they were married and at home, he said, "Darling, you must understand about me that I'm awkward with feelings, and, really, that's the reason why I can't use words to express them."

"I do," she said.

"Listen to me, please, darling, because I may never be able to talk to you in this way again, which I have to admit

I've been preparing myself for. You must believe that I love you, and always shall, and that's a principle."

She said, "Do you like poetry?"

"I do."

She smiled and said, "I'd like to go out into the garden with you."

"In the rain?"

"The roses look so beautiful in the rain."

He stood and looked at his desk and said, "I must return to my work."

"Then when you've finished."

"Come back in an hour."

She sighed and quietly said she would, and she drew the plaid from her, folded it neatly, and left the room as he returned to his desk; she quietly closed the double doors.

She went back an hour later, dressed and carrying a large umbrella. Tim was slumped forward on his desk, in the midst of papers. He was asleep. But she felt something more for him than his dedication to his work; she felt, seeing him there asleep, the helplessness in him in the world that she felt was not his, that she was sure he had little or no faith in.

As soon as she tapped him on a shoulder, he sat straight up, wide awake, and looked at the papers on his desk, then at her, and frowned a little.

"We're going into the garden," she said, "and I've brought an umbrella."

Still frowning a little, he looked at his desk, then at her.

She said, "Come on."

"Very well," he said, "for a moment, then I have to get back here."

And out in the garden, she did remark on the smell of the mass of roses in the rain, but he said nothing, and she asked herself if she was overdoing her attention, which was meant for him.

The house of Tim's parents, in St. John's Wood, was closer to what Nancy had imagined Tim's house to be: it had clarity and space, and the parquet floors shone in the light through the tall, wide, many-paned windows, their inside wooden shutters folded back to let the sunlight in. The pictures were old-master prints.

Mrs. Arbib, her hair parted and combed back into a chignon, wore a stark black dress, her husband a dark suit, the buttoned jacket a little cinched in at the waist. Mrs. Arbib's very dark eyes seemed to embrace Nancy sadly, bringing her into a world of sorrow with a frail embrace and soft kisses on both her cheeks. She stood back while her husband held out his arms to Nancy just enough to grasp her elbows and said, "Welcome to London."

Mrs. Arbib poured tea, which a maid passed around, then brought little diamonds of baklava on fine china plates with fine silver forks. The tea napkins were white linen with crocheted lace around the edges.

Nothing in the room suggested where Mr. and Mrs. Arbib were from, and even their accents, though not English, could have been formed by any number of languages, as, no doubt, they were.

"Tell me about Alexandria," Nancy said. "I really want to know."

Smiling a slightly ironical smile, Mr. Arbib said, "Alexandria has a long, long history." He seemed to be announcing that Alexandria had a longer history than any history Nancy could claim.

"I was born in Cairo," Mrs. Arbib said. "Cairo has even a longer history than Alexandria."

Her chin raised, Nancy asked her, "What do you remember most of Cairo?"

"You'll laugh. When I was a little girl, out for a walk with my English nanny, I was fascinated by the way the men in the laundries who ironed would take water into their mouths and spray it out over the sheet or shirt or whatever they were ironing to dampen it. Now, why do I remember that?" Nancy showed off a little, saying, "My mother had lovely memories of Berlin."

She had the sudden sense of being in the wrong place here in London, in the wrong place with Tim's parents, in the wrong place with Tim. There was no Vinnie around who would listen to her say she found Mrs. Arbib, for all her apparent solemnity, a slightly silly woman. And as for Mr Arbib, wasn't he slightly too seriously pretentious?

The tea things were cleared away, but Tim remained to talk lightly about a recent auction of old-master etchings. Nancy considered herself well educated, not only by college but by her parents, but she did not know the artists referred to by the Arbibs, and she began to tire from having to pay attention to a conversation she didn't understand and wasn't interested in, talk, between Tim and his father, about how much the collection was worth.

She asked to look at the pictures, which couldn't have been a better way to ingratiate herself with Tim's father;

with a hand held out graciously, he showed her to a dead white wall on which etchings hung one above another in thin black frames. Nancy exclaimed, in a slightly affected voice, "There's a Piranesi, I love Piranesi"—one she recognized because the etching was of his fantastic prisons—but she did not know who Giulio Carpioni was, or Michele Marieschi, or Giuseppe Zocchi, about whom Mr. Arbib knew a lot.

Mr. Arbib said, "We have been able to keep the collection together, but I can't say for how much longer."

The collection made Nancy think of the Arbibs as refugees in London, and she wondered if they mingled with no one but other refugees from Egypt.

When they were sitting again, Mrs. Arbib asked Nancy what she had read at university, and she answered that she had her degree in literature. She had concentrated on the works of Henry James.

Mr. Arbib pressed a knuckle against his chin and said his favorite writer was Somerset Maugham.

The doorbell rang, and Nancy was introduced to friends of the family, two men and a woman, who had arrived to play music in the sitting room. They came regularly, Mr. Arbib told Nancy, and would stay on for what Mrs. Arbib called a simple supper.

Listening to the trio, Nancy saw Tim raise a hand—a poised hand—to touch a cheek with an index finger. Yes, he was handsome, in profile sharply angled, his close-cropped hair clearly defined at his nape, at his sideburns, along the receding hairline, his head seemingly set into his stiff white collar with its carefully knotted tie. And though he looked

severe, he had a right to his severity, because he was supe-
rior not only intellectually but emotionally, for here, now,
listening to the rapturous music, he was at the highest level
of emotion, higher than she would ever be able to go, higher for no greater outward expression than a finger touching
his cheek.

While the piano kept up an insistent, slowly repeated
rhythm, the stringed instruments seemed to rise up from
and float above the piano to a height of great, swooning
freedom, and she rose up there with that swooning music.
Tim, lowering his hand, turned to her and smiled a smile
that she understood was a recognition that she, too, was on
the high level, where she was accepted, and where, yes, she
was loved. He turned again to the trio. He would not have
used the word love any more than anyone could use one
word to describe the feelings roused by the music, but for
the duration of the movement she felt an expansiveness
that longed to be called love, however much she thought
she could not use a word that Tim would not use.

She assured herself that everything was going to be all
right. Everything would come together, and coming together would make it all whole. She longed above all for that: for
everything to come together and be whole.

She found herself swaying a little, and stopped.

Leaving, Tim said to her, "My parents told me how
much they like you."

At home—what she felt must be her home—he told her
to go up to their bedroom and sleep, she was exhausted. He
would go to his study alone for an hour or so at his desk.

Alone, Nancy tried to sustain the sense of wholeness, as

if the sense could be sustained by intention long enough for her to fall asleep and wake up next to Tim, in bed beside her, holding her.

She always slept in the morning after Tim got up, but before he left for the law courts he did wake her enough to tell her to go on sleeping, he wanted her to have all the rest she needed for their child.

When she had a miscarriage she said, "You'll want to divorce me."

"Of course I'll not divorce you," he insisted. "The fact is you can become pregnant, and you'll become pregnant again, and you'll carry the baby to term. This, I am certain, is a certainty."

But she didn't believe him; she never believed what he said to her, and she never believed what she said to him.

Nancy at first thought the invitation cards Tim placed on the mantelpiece—what he called the chimneypiece—were pretentious, but she thought she had to allow Tim his pretensions. Then, in the sitting rooms of homes they were invited to for dinner parties, she saw invitation cards displayed on the mantels of other fireplaces, and thought that what she had taken to be a pretentious display of social connections—some of the cards had raised gold crests on them—was actually an English custom. One evening, she found on the mantelpiece a large invitation card from someone she had never heard of to a charity event to raise money for music in country churches: a famous pianist was to play in the presence of Their Royal Highnesses the Duke

and Duchess of Kent at the Middle Temple, Champagne
7:00 p.m. Recital 7:30 p.m. Supper 8:30 p.m., Carriages at
10:30 p.m., Black Tie. She picked it up.

Tim came in with a silver salver of champagne flutes
and an open bottle.

"When did this come?" she asked.

"In this morning's post."

"I don't know the person who's inviting."

"But I do."

"What are 'carriages at 10:30'?" Nancy asked.

"We've got to be out by 10:30."

"That doesn't seem polite."

He laughed a rough laugh. "Would you rather they rang
a bell and shouted that it was time, as in a pub?"

Tim filled a flute and handed it to Nancy. She said, "I
guess I'm just beginning to learn what it is to be English."

Not waiting for her, Tim drank, then said, "You'll never
be English. Nor will I. I'm not English. I'm a Jew."

The early autumn evening when they were to go to the
Middle Temple was hot. Nancy liked to take a long time to
bathe and make up and dress, but by the time she was sitting on the bed, putting on her shoes, Tim had not yet come
home to change into his black tie. Because of the heat, the
window of the bedroom was open onto the back garden.
She was putting on her second shoe when Tim came into
the room, taking off his suit jacket, and said, frowning,
"You're not wearing stockings."

She raised a bare leg and lifted the skirt of her long,
tight, black dress to admire her calf and ankle, and she
moved her shoe from side to side. "Don't you like the look

of my leg?" she asked. She badly needed to joke with him because, really, it was ridiculous that he didn't approve of her not wearing stockings. He would never have approved of the casual way she had dressed in New York.

He grasped one of her ankles. Startled, she began to lose balance, and threw out her arms and shouted, "Tim." He raised her leg higher, and she fell backward onto the bed. He let go.

"Put on stockings," he said.

She was still too startled to know what he meant. She asked, "Stockings?"

"You are not going to that party with your legs bare."

Her dress was rucked under her and her bare legs were exposed. One shoe had fallen off.

"It's too hot for stockings," she said.

He appeared, suddenly, to expand, his head to become larger, his shoulders broader, his chest deeper, his hips wider, his raised hand huge, but it was particularly his head, with thick black hair and the dark shaved beard shadowing his white skin, that became so large it shocked her. His voice was equal to his size.

He shouted, "You had fucking well better get up from that bed and put on stockings."

Stunned, she sat still for a while and noted there was a patch high on one of his cheeks where he hadn't shaved his beard. Slowly she got up from the bed and, with one shoe on and one off, she limped to a bureau, opened a drawer, took out a crumpled pair of panty hose, and held it out to him. "Will this do?" she asked.

"It will do." But he kept watching her as she took off

her shoe, hitched up the skirt of her dress, pulled off her underpants, and, all her lower body exposed, drew on the panty hose.

She asked, "Should I wear a hat?"

"A hat will not be necessary," he said.

They wouldn't go by car, Tim said, but taxi, and, without asking why, Nancy simply followed him, clutching a little purse covered with black jet beads. In the taxi, as if nothing had happened between them, he told her, as he told her every evening, about his day in chambers. She listened but said nothing.

When they got out of the taxi and Tim was paying, the driver asked, smiling, "Important do this evening?" Tim grunted, all he would allow in response to the taxi driver, and Nancy, to make up for her husband, said to the taxi driver, "Come on in for a glass of champagne," which made Tim smile at her, and he took her by the arm. Tim approved of her solicitude. She did want Tim's approval.

The Middle Temple had stone-paved passages with polished wood-paneled walls and portraits of men in old frames. Just within the entrance was a round table holding place cards arranged in circles to indicate at what tables and in what rooms people would sit for supper. Tim looked for his name and hers. After he found them, he continued to study the seating of the guests. Then she followed him down a wooden staircase with a thick wooden banister and a red runner patterned with large blue flowers out into a garden where men and women in evening dress were gathered along a stone parapet, a wide, deep lawn extending beyond the parapet. A waiter came with a tray to offer Tim and Nancy flutes of champagne from a silver tray.

There was nothing for Nancy to do but be social. Tim introduced her to Christopher Swire, a young, bald man with large black eyes who had organized and was paying for the party, who stood before them for a silent moment before looking beyond; without excusing himself, he went off to speak to another couple standing near by.

Tim said to Nancy, "Really, Christopher only gives a do like this to be able to invite the Royals."

Nancy looked around for the Royals.

"We'd better go up to the recital hall," Tim said. "The seats are unreserved."

The hall was large, with a groined ceiling and high, wood-paneled walls, and painted on every wooden panel was a coat of arms. Along a high shelf that went all round the hall were placed breastplates and helmets.

Tim saw his old friend from his Oxford days, Toby Tonks, who had been best man at the wedding in New York. Toby kissed Nancy on both cheeks, and she sat between him and Tim, who talked to one another past her.

Tim, shocked, said, "Toby, you're wearing a clip-on bow tie."

Toby touched his tie.

"In our Oxford days you wouldn't have been caught dead wearing a clip-on bow tie."

The pianist came in, sat at the grand piano, adjusted the height of the stool by turning knobs on either side of it, and then held his fingers over the keys for a moment before he struck the first chord. All the while he played, people in the audience coughed.

Nancy got through the supper, seated between two men whose names she hadn't been told. Acting to amuse them, with sassy sensuality she knew how to project, she touched their arms to make a point and shook her breasts a little when she laughed. They were barristers, and she told them she thought the law should be reformed to allow women to batter their husbands, even to castrate their husbands, and, seeing that the more outrageous she was the more they liked it, to murder their husbands. Both men were sweating. Tim was sitting across from her at the round table, and whenever the barristers laughed she saw him look toward her and smile and nod to let her know he was pleased that she was doing such a good job.

She was deliberately acting out of her own character, and thought she was having her little revenge on him for forcing her to wear stockings on a hot night by impersonating an American seductress. Tim didn't seem to sense this, but she knew how to get the better of him by being a social flirt in a world he had once told her he couldn't properly behave in because he did not know how to be social, but had to rely on her.

While acting, Nancy saw through the people at the table, and what she saw, to her own strange awareness, was that there was no darkness behind these people. Shouldn't she prefer being among people who had no darkness behind them? It did amuse her in some way that they lacked deep character because they were without darkness, for darkness behind a person authenticated that person's character. She would make her home among these characterless people. She would be as amusingly superficial as they—would learn their habits of speech, would smile the vague smile of a duchess at people she didn't know. She would even learn to know her place as a Jew, a place that at home she was never sure of—that being to consider herself privileged to be accepted and to appreciate the privilege, and always, always to be amusing.

Married to Tim, she would become British, and that would make her different. She would learn something about irony, irony about the British, who took delight in irony, and, too, irony about the United States, an un-ironical country.

And this was what was wrong with Yvon, she thought; he had no sense of irony, none.

Napkins falling to the floor from laps, everyone rose when the Royals, the duchess at one table and the duke at another, got up. The duchess, her eyes wide and staring apparently at nothing, walked through the standing guests, and, still apparently without seeing anything as she stared, stopped for a second before a woman and smiled a smile that seemed to float out from her face and have nothing to do with her. The woman curtsied. Then, as soon as the Royals had left, the guests dispersed, as if in a hurry to get away.

Nancy on his arm, Tim left when Toby did, and all together they walked for a while in the cool outside air after the stifling inside.

Toby said, "I was a long way from being seated at the best table."

Tim said, "I would put our table at, say, fifth best."

"Not too bad."

Nancy laughed. She could not, before she married, have imagined herself in so totally different a world, a world that, for all its being foreign, did not seem so much strange as it was merely peculiar. She was in a world in which she could come to terms with the manners, could find out what carriages at ten thirty meant, find out that men shouldn't wear clip-on bow ties, could learn, maybe, how to curtsy.

She'd married Tim, and maybe—or to use the English word, perhaps—she wondered why she had, but as much as Tim insisted he was not English, would never be English, he did, and now she did, live in an English world. With Tim, she thought, she would be free of fantasies she only now realized she had to grow out of—free, oh, of longings, a word she had to be free of. With Tim she was free to act in a world where he allowed her to act for him, who was bad at acting but admired her ability, and free to help him. And, as remarkable as this seemed to her when she first thought it, there was nothing, finally, unknowable about him.

Nancy sat close to Tim in the back seat of the taxi. He reached out to put an arm around her. "You were splendid," he said.

"Was I?"

"You were," he said. "Thank you, darling. You were tru-ly splendid."

She did what she felt was still out of character: she put her head on his shoulder, and she thought she would show him some feeling for his dependence on her, though he didn't seem to have noticed that his wife had made a little bit of a fool of herself. She had done it for him, and it had pleased him.

She gave way to his wanting to make love that night, hold-ing his head as if to steady him, and she wished, for him, that she would become pregnant again. His lovemaking had more consideration for her than she had known, and she thought he was now considering her as his wife, the wife who would bear a family for him, and she responded as his wife, a response that made her feel, perhaps, loving, if she allowed herself to use the word "loving" even to herself.

Before turning away from her, he said, "I'm sorry, darling, for my fit of anger earlier. I honestly don't know where the anger comes from. I can't imagine my father ever treating my mother in that way, so it must be something that has come to me living in England."

"Well," she said, "I guess you have to think yourself back into being Jewish, because Jews never get angry."

He laughed and kissed her and turned over and switched off the lamp on his side of the bed.

He fell asleep, but she seemed to be seeing at a distance, far beyond the room, and out there snow began to fall, and she saw Yvon walking towards her through the deepening snow, Yvon from a long way away—she had no idea from how far away; and he stopped when he saw her.

Surprised, he said, Nancy.

She asked, Where have you been?

He smiled and said, Oh, lots of places.

In America, she asked?

All over America, he said, all over this country.

What were you doing all over?

Collecting specimens of rocks.

And are you happy now?

No, not really, but that doesn't matter. He smiled a wider smile and said, I won't ever be happy, because, you see, I was born unhappy.

Ah, she said, Yvon, and, as if pleading, called out to him to come closer, Yvon.

But as he was walking away in the falling snow, he asked, And you, are you happy?

No, she answered, no, I'm not.

He disappeared in the snow, and she was left with an overwhelming sense of longing.

She was in her bedroom brushing her hair in front of the full-length mirror. She had not redecorated the room as she once thought she would. Reflected in the mirror she could see behind her part of the bedroom wall, a curtain, and half a window, and outside the window a plane tree in sunlight, its leaves going faintly brown-yellow. She focused on the tree in the mirror, not herself, when she noticed a blue pigeon perched on a branch; the sense came to her that someone was standing behind her, just where the mirror didn't reflect, and the moment she thought this she felt that this person was about to grab her and pull her backward. Startled, her brush raised and her hair flying, she turned. No one was there. As soon as she finished brushing her hair, she went downstairs to find Tim.

She came into the sitting room while Tim was on the telephone, the telephone receiver in the crook of his neck and a tiny agenda, soft leather with gilt-edged paper and a silk page keeper, in his hands. He said, over the receiver, "Let me see," and turned the pages of the agenda. Nancy was uncertain if he wanted her in the room while he was on the telephone, and the way he looked at her gave no indication whether he wanted her to stay or go. He said, "No, no, next week won't do." Maybe ("maybe," Nancy thought, or "perhaps") he was speaking to one of his friends from his Oxford days. Tim had been at Christ Church at Oxford, and a lot of his friends were also from Oxford, and he saw them on his own. But Nancy heard Tim say, "Yes, the week after will do for Nancy and me, that will do, but let me check." He turned the pages of his little agenda and said, "No, no, wait, it won't do, I see I've penciled in dinner, and we're waiting to hear if it's on or not. But the weekend after that, I see, is perfectly free." As Nancy was turning to leave the sitting room, leaving it up to Tim to make whatever plans he wanted, excluding or including her, he waved his agenda at her to stay. He spoke a little more over the telephone, smiling broadly, and when he hung up he said, "We're going to the Kesses in Scotland."

"Who are the Kesses?" Nancy asked.

"Hilary and James Kess, old friends I've wanted you to meet. They'll like you, you'll see," he said, but he spoke as if he wasn't sure they would, as if their liking her or not was not up to them, but up to her. He said, "I'm counting on you," and she tried to imagine these people who meant something to Tim that she didn't understand, and whom Tim insisted she must like. She had no choice. James Kess was a retired judge.

* * *

They took the train to Scotland first class, and changed at Keswick for a local to Dumfries in the Lowlands. They arrived by taxi over the narrow, dark country roads at the Kesses' Victorian brick castle with a neo-Gothic porch, a crenellated tower, and narrow, pointed, leaded windows. James and Hilary met their guests in the hall, which had a high coffered wooden ceiling and uneven stone flagging.

Hilary Kess said immediately that there was cold salmon in the kitchen, and led the way. She stopped at two long grooves worn into the flagging of the passage and said, "These were caused by the wheels of the tea trolley being pushed into the drawing room and back into the kitchen for years and years."

Nancy admired the grooves in the stone.

She was never really introduced to the Kesses by Tim, but she supposed that didn't matter, because they knew who she was and she knew who they were, and perhaps in England it wasn't done to introduce people one already knew by name.

In the kitchen, at a long deal table set with china plates on the bare wood and blue napkins printed with tiny white flowers and crystal wine and water glasses and silver and, at the center, the cold, skinned salmon surrounded by slices of cucumber, they sat to eat. Nancy saw how pleased Hilary and James were to have Tim with them, and, if they paid less attention to her than to him, she understood they were closer to him and that there were reasons for their closeness that had to do with James' past profession and Tim's present profession, and even if they didn't talk about this, they were both in a world that was as complicated as the making of dates, and she, who had never found making a date complicated, was still outside of that world, a world of names that Hilary recognized. James Kess kept filling their glasses with white wine.

Distracted from the talk, Nancy noted that in the kitchen was a large range with many ovens, and an overstuffed sofa was set before the range.

Addressing Nancy for the first time since she and Tim had arrived, Hilary said to her, "It was noble of you to come all this way to meet us."

Nancy laughed a little. "Oh," she said, not sure how to deal with the extravagance, "I don't know how noble I am."

"No, no," Hilary said, "I mean just how noble you are for coming, far, far beyond the call of duty. I'm sure we're going to have the grandest time all together, however catch as catch can it will be, because, I must tell you, we haven't planned to account for each and every one of your minutes here with entertainments. We rather let our guests do what they want. Isn't that why you like coming, Tim, because you can do here just exactly as you want?"

Tim said to her, "My reasons for coming here are multiple."

It could be, Nancy thought, that one of Tim's reasons for coming was that he wanted to become a judge.

Hilary said to Nancy, "We leave you, shamelessly, to your devices, while we, without you, get on with all the boring bits we have to get on with. You won't mind getting your own breakfast on Sunday morning when we skip off to church? We go because, really, we're not native to the place, and we think it helps us, in a hokey-pokey way, with the locals if they see us in church."

Hokey-pokey? Nancy wondered, staring at Hilary, who seemed to be waiting for her to speak. It occurred to Nancy to offer to go to church with the Kesses, but then she thought maybe, or perhaps, not.

Nancy asked, "Where are you from, then?"

"London," James said. "And we thought we'd move as far away as possible from the Old Bailey and the London world of law when I retired."

"And here we are," Hilary said, "trying to fit in, higgledy-piggledy, with the locals, and, of course, always, but always, getting things wrong."

"But not as wrong as our recent American guest who offended everyone by wearing a plaid tie when we went to dine at a neighbor's house," James said. He laughed, a shrugging laugh. "I was wicked. I didn't tell him, when I saw his bright tartan tie, just how much he would offend. I am wicked."

"Oh, but they weren't really offended, not really. I didn't think so," Hilary said. "Really, they took it all in good humor after all, and even promised our American friend they'd set him up with his own tartan."

"Of course they never would," James said.

As they walked from the kitchen into the hall, Hilary said, "Whenever I wear tartan, I make sure it's the Royal Stewart, which is the Queen's, and which all her subjects are entitled to wear."

"I see," Nancy said.

They sat before the neo-Gothic stone fireplace in big, dark leather armchairs and a big, dark leather sofa in the hall. A suit of armor, rusty about the edges, stood against a frayed, hanging tapestry. James offered to light the fire, but Tim said it wasn't really necessary: it wasn't cold and he and Nancy would go to bed soon. Hilary told James to offer brandy if he wasn't going to light the fire.

James said to Nancy, "The armor has nothing to do with ancestry, not Hilary's or mine, at any rate."

"Nor the castle, not that it is anything like an ancestral castle," Hilary said. "Goodness, I don't have any ancestry to brag about, I want to make that perfectly clear; nor, really, does James. James wanted to leave London, so we looked through *Country Life* for places, and took a liking to this from a photograph. It wasn't expensive and didn't need much work. We moved in during the summer, and what we didn't know was how bitterly cold and rainy it would be for most of the rest of the year."

James said, "And even in the summer it's often cold and rainy."

"It was sunny today," Nancy said.

"Freakish," Hilary said. "Most of the year we live in the kitchen, where it's cozy. We sit on the lovely, chintzy sofa in front of the Aga and doze."

"In fact," James said. "It's terrible here, terrible. It's rainy and cold all the time."

Hilary said she had invited George and Constance Plummerton the next day, Sunday, for lunch. They, too, had moved to Scotland from London, but, Hilary said, like herself and James, there wasn't anything Scottish in them. George was English, and Constance was mostly Welsh.

Nancy thought she was beginning to hear different accents, and it occurred to her that Hilary's accent was not English—not, anyway, of a class that Tim had learned at school, or so Nancy assumed. But she wouldn't ask Hilary where she was from originally.

Holding a snifter of brandy by the base and swirling the brandy in it, Tim said to Nancy, "He's Sir George."

She said, "I'll remember that."

Hilary said, "He was knighted, but, you know, he was an

Hon., born an Hon.—really more distinguished than to be knighted."

"What was George knighted for?" Tim asked.

So, Nancy noted, Tim didn't call him Sir George, as he told her to; he said George.

"You don't know? I'm surprised. For his English bicycles," James said.

Tim jerked his head back and said, "Of course, of course," then repeated, "of course," so Nancy realized that he hadn't known.

Nancy, who felt that they were all playing a game they didn't take seriously, said, "I had an English three-speed bicycle when I was growing up in America. Everyone I knew had to have an English three-speed bicycle."

James said, "George was knighted for exporting them to America, where, just as you say, you and everyone you knew had to have one, which meant that lots of American dollars came in exchange to the United Kingdom. He made the United Kingdom richer, and he became very rich, and he became Sir George."

Tim said, "George once told me that at a fancy do such as an embassy dinner he knows, just by looking around at the others present during drinks beforehand, where, by protocol, he will be seated. He said he's never wrong."

Hilary suggested to Nancy that the ladies retire and leave the men to talk, given how much James liked to talk with Tim. James smiled at Nancy and said quietly, "Tim's a clever young man."

Tim said, "I hope the recognition of that is one of the reasons my wife had for marrying me."

Nancy said, "Of course it was."

"His cleverness won't disappoint you," Hilary said to Nancy.

All Nancy could think of to say, meekly and in appreciation of being so lucky to be married to a man whose cleverness supposedly wouldn't disappoint her, was, "Thank you."

Taking Nancy's hand as though to reassure her, Hilary said to Tim, "I'm not at all sure I should introduce George and Constance to Nancy as Sir George and Lady Plummerton. I don't have a butler, but open the door myself. We're really quite informal, in a rather tinkerty-tonk way. It would be awkward, in the midst of our informality, to be so formal. And how would I introduce Nancy, if all the rest of us go by first names, as Mrs. Arbib?" She let go of Nancy's hand.

"I see the difficulty," Tim said.

"Then don't call anyone anything," James said.

"There is that," Hilary said.

In their bedroom alone, while Tim was using the bath down the passage, Nancy held a drawn curtain aside to look out a leaded window to black pine trees against the deep gray sky, and she felt the pull to look behind her, and she glanced back into the room, at the bed with high posts and a large wardrobe.

And this came over her: grief, the word itself a revelation, as she had never before thought it applied to her so deeply, especially now, here in this large, cold house with people she didn't want to know, with a husband she was suddenly afraid to know.

She asked herself how she would act as Tim would expect her the next day, and she got into bed, under the heavy blankets. When Tim, in pajamas and a towel over an arm, came into the room, she turned away.

He said, "I really would have expected Hilary to know how to introduce you to Constance Plummerton. Constance, may I introduce Nancy. And Nancy Arbib, Lady Plummerton. But it would be as vulgar of me to tell her as it would to correct her idiotic usage of idiotic expressions. It never occurred to me quite as much before that she's Australian, and childish, rather."

When he was in bed next to her, she said, "Please switch off the light."

In the morning, while James and Hilary were at church, Tim and Nancy took a walk wearing gum boots. The autumn day was sunny. The sharp, flinty hills were dark green, and on them, isolated, were one-story stone houses painted white, the stone doorways and window frames bright blue or red or green.

They walked along a river. A rotting sheep stood upright in the current, the clear water swirling around its exposed skull.

In the high distance, the castle, as they walked back to it, appeared to have a cloud gathering about it in the sunlight. Tim and Nancy joined Hilary and James in the hall to wait for their guests. Hilary kept twisting her pearl necklace. She said, "I hear a car," and quickly went to the door and opened it. An elderly woman in a cardigan and a high-necked jersey and woolen trousers came in and Hilary kissed her on both cheeks, and then an elderly gentleman, in a pullover that looked too big for him, one of the wings of his tie-less collar under the V neck and one out, and Hilary kissed him on both cheeks. And after James and Tim kissed the woman and shook the hand of the man, Hilary, smiling more widely and gesturing with one hand to present her grandly, said, "This is Tim's wife." Hilary did not call the woman and man anything. They both said to Nancy, "How do you do," and Nancy held out her hand, but as soon as she did she realized it hadn't occurred to the woman and man to do the same, perhaps because they'd assumed it wouldn't have been expected, and just as Nancy was lowering her hand they stepped forward with their hands extended toward her. Embarrassed, Hilary laughed.

She said, "Now that we're all happily together, we'll go into the drawing room for sherry, which I'm sure you're all passionate for."

Why now, in the drawing room rather than the hall, Nancy wondered, except, perhaps, for a fire in the fireplace that heated the room, while a fire in the hall would not have heated even the hearth.

At a table set with bottles and glasses under another frayed tapestry, James did the honors with the drinks. No one had sherry except Nancy, who, because Hilary had said they would have sherry, supposed that that was what she should have.

Hilary said to Sir George and Lady Plummerton, "You really are noble, braving this dreary day to come to us."

"Isn't it sunny today?" Lady Plummerton asked.

"It won't last," Hilary said. "We'll see, only too sadly, how dreary the day will get."

Tim asked the couple how Augusta was, and they said

she was having a delightful time, and they should, really, have been annoyed at her ringing every day from so far away, which was frightfully expensive, but they were, after all, reassured to know she was quite all right out there.

"Who's Augusta?" Nancy asked.

"Our daughter," replied Lady Plummerton, not quite looking at Nancy, maybe, Nancy thought, because she was shy.

"And where is she?"

"Mombasa," Sir George said, and he also seemed too shy to look at Nancy as he spoke. "Africa, you know."

"Remember that story about Africa Lord Fairley used to tell," Tim said, "about an uncle of his coming back to England from some African colony with a lion cub, which, on the high seas, fell overboard, and, as the captain refused to stop for a lion cub, the uncle jumped over the railing to save it, knowing he would stop for a marquis."

Blinking rapidly, Lady Plummerton said, "No, I don't remember."

Tim laughed and said, "And then the cub grew up into a fully developed lion, which the family kept on the grounds of their country house, and one day it ate the uncle." Tim drank. "Well, the lion was given to the London Zoo, and Lord Fairley remembered being taken by his aunt to see the lion that ate his uncle."

Sir George said, "We didn't know Lord Fairley."

"I am sorry," Tim said.

"Not at all," Sir George said.

Nancy asked him, "What is your daughter doing in Mombasa?"

Lady Plummerton said, "She did something rather silly—we never understood why—and after she recovered a bit and thought she'd like to get away, she chose Mombasa."

Looking into the distance, Sir George said quietly, "She can be very silly."

Nancy thought she hadn't understood them—they couldn't be so open and blithe that they were telling her, someone they hadn't even been introduced to, that their daughter had tried to kill herself. Repeating the expression Lady Plummerton had used, but with a tone of incredulity that asked, please, for an explanation of something she couldn't have understood, she asked, "She tried to do herself in?"

"I'm afraid so," Lady Plummerton said, blinking, not looking directly at Nancy.

Nancy saw Tim frowning at her, and she knew that she mustn't ask anything more about Augusta. Maybe, she thought, their being so open about their daughter precluded anyone asking anything more than what they had stated.

Sir George tried to smile when he said, "We hope she doesn't return with a lion cub that will grow up to eat us."

Hilary said, "I should think we're all desperate to eat," and suggested they go to the dining room.

Lunch was at a round table in the dining room, not at the table in the kitchen. Sir George sat on Hilary's right, next to him sat Nancy, and then James, then Lady Plummerton, and, completing the circle, Tim, on Hilary's left. Tim smiled at Nancy across the table, and there was some expectation from her in the smile.

Hilary rang a little bell, and an old man wearing black

tie came in carrying a bowl of rice and mushrooms. Sir George leaned back in his chair and, raising his hand in a salute, said, "How are you, Arthur?" to which the old man said, "Keeping well, sir." Arthur held the bowl, a little shakily, for the guests, all casual in their sweaters, not one man wearing a tie.

When he left, Hilary said, "Without any kind of permanent help, I don't know what I'd do without Arthur coming in from time to time."

"What would any of us do?" Lady Plummerton asked.

"Last week, he helped me hang the curtains in my sitting room."

"He's especially good with hanging curtains," Hilary said.

"Who is Arthur?" Nancy asked.

Sir George said, "Arthur? You mean, there is someone in the world who doesn't know who Arthur is? Arthur is a Polish refugee from the war who landed in the village, and has been here longer than any of us."

"And we're all dependent on him," James said.

Arthur came in with the bowl of rice and mushrooms again for second helpings.

Nancy listened to the others at the table talk and laugh about people she had never heard of; no one bothered to explain to her who they were. She heard names—Clarissa and Robert and Alicia and Humphrey—but she had no idea how these names related to one another, and the conversation was too involved for her to break in and ask who was who, or if, she wondered, she should break in and ask. No one addressed her or even looked at her to include her in what was being said, with such hilarity, about Clarissa and

Robert and Alicia and Humphrey.

Nancy thought it was up to her to take part, but the only way she could, without spoiling the fun by asking for explanations, was to laugh when they laughed, though she didn't know what she was laughing about. Tim, who had pleaded with her to help him in social gatherings, appeared to be just where he wanted to be.

Nancy kept thinking of their daughter Augusta.

Hilary said, "We'll go back to the drawing room for coffee, which I'm sure you're all frantic for."

No, Nancy thought, Hilary can't be English.

The drawing room had French windows that gave onto a lawn and a stone wall; beyond the stone wall the land rose and fell, gray-green, under a gray sky. As they entered the room, Hilary, drawn to the windows, said, "Hounds." Nancy, too, went to the windows and saw a pack of hounds, their noses to the ground and their tongues out, running across a gray-green misty field toward a row of dark pines. Hilary said, "You see, the hounds are tonguing the air. I've learned all this sort of thing, not that I ever get it right, but I go along, making my way." After the hounds came the mounted hunters. "We'll know when they've killed the fox," Hilary said. "We'll hear it."

Wild barking came from beyond the pines.

Nancy heard herself say, "How horrible," and it was only when the room went silent that she realized everyone had heard her.

When the barking stopped, Hilary turned away from Nancy and, looking about the room, folded her hands together and said, "Well now, more coffee for anyone?"

Sir George said he would, and Lady Plummerton said

she wouldn't, but that they really should be going. However, Sir George held out his cup to Hilary, and, with it filled, he went to Nancy, still standing at the windows. She looked out as he approached her.

Quietly, he said to her, "If I didn't think I had to, I wouldn't do it. Fox hunting is barbaric, but, then, the British are barbaric."

She said, "Sir George, I'm a foreigner here."

"Please call me George," he said, "if you'll allow me to call you—" He paused.

"Nancy."

"Yes, of course—Nancy."

After Sir George and Lady Plummerton left, James said Hilary must have a rest, she absolutely must, and Hilary, laughing as if she must give in to him, said to Tim and Nancy, "What can I do now but have a rest?"

"We'll see you for tea," James said.

As soon as James and Hilary went, leaving Tim and Nancy alone in the drawing room, Tim frowned at Nancy in a way that made her draw back a little. But she followed him up to their room, and as soon as their door was shut, Tim's entire body, and particularly his head, expanded with sudden rage. He shouted, "What the fuck do you know about fox hunting? You humiliated me before my friends."

Nancy sat on the bed. "Your bloody friends."

"And I'll thank you not to use the word bloody, which, you obviously do not know, is offensive in this country. You shouldn't use offensive language to describe people in whose company you should considered yourself honored to be."

"What you don't know is Sir George came up to me and

agreed and said it was barbaric and that if he weren't English he wouldn't hunt."

"There you see. He was being polite. A gentleman."

"Anyway, Sir George and Lady Plummerton did not ask me one direct question, not one."

Tim breathed in deeply. "You need to understand why they didn't ask you questions." Tim put on a professional voice to explain. "Because, by the mere fact of your being among us at an intimate luncheon party, everyone's assumption is that you are known to everyone, and such questions could only make you feel you don't belong."

"But they didn't know anything about me."

"Let me try again. I realize it's rather subtle. They didn't ask you questions about your life because your being among us meant they should have known everything, and they didn't want to offend you by asking questions that would have revealed they didn't. Do you understand anything of what I'm saying?"

She asked, "Why are you trying to make stupid excuses for the English?"

"What do you know about being English?"

"What do you know?" she shouted. "You yourself told me, you're a Jew."

Tim swung his arm out and back and hit her with the back of his hand on the side of her face, and she fell backward onto the bed.

The blow did not leave a mark, but James and Hilary knew from Nancy's stunned look that something had happened, and at tea, the elderly couple were attentive to her.

When Hilary left her side on the sofa James took her

place. He seemed to have had his little talk prepared when he said to Nancy, "I want to tell you something about London." James leaned toward her and smiled a little. "Many people, the British included, imagine there is a center to London where, if they can only get to it, they will be established forever. They may think that being invited to dine at the Coffees' house puts them at the center, but they find, when, at another dinner party at the Teas, they let it be known that just last week they dined at the house of the Coffees, that the Teas will say, 'My God, you didn't! The Coffees are the most boring people in the world,' and they will think they made a terrible mistake and the center was not at the Coffees but at the Teas. And then, the next week, when, at the Cocoas, they let it drop that they are on such good terms with the Teas that they have been invited for the weekend, the Cocoas will say, 'Not the Teas! My God, how can you bear the Teas?' and they will think, again, that they have made a terrible mistake, and, really, the center is at the Cocoas. And this will go on and on in that way until they are invited to Buckingham Palace to dine with the queen, who they are absolutely sure is the center, and will drop this bit of information when they meet the Horlickses at a reception, and the Horlickses tell them they consider the queen a Hanoverian arriviste and they won't have anything to do with her socially."

Tim, holding a cup of tea, laughed.

Without looking at him, James continued to Nancy, "I think this is something even Tim, who purports to understand everything about London, does not understand."

Tim put down his cup and laughed louder.

In bed, waiting for Tim, Nancy felt grief, grief for whom or for what she didn't know, come over her again, and she rose from the bed and went to the window and watched the crows in the pine trees.

Nancy became pregnant again, then had another miscarriage. Tim was made very anxious by this, and said over and over that something had to be done. In his anxiety he blamed their doctor, and threatened to bring a suit for malpractice. She said sadly but calmly, "Please don't," and he set his jaw. She was made deeply sad by the miscarriage, sad not only because the choice to be a mother was taken away from her, but because she believed she would have been a good mother.

She put on weight, more than when she'd been pregnant. Her white, finely freckled breasts bulged in her bra, and her hips expanded and rounded.

She thought she must, for Tim's sake, become pregnant again. She did, and Tim's anxiety left him, but she had another miscarriage. Again he shouted that something would be done, something had to be done. She stood calmly and listened to him. She would do anything, anything he said she must do, but, in herself, as though accepting what she knew was beyond her control, she accepted that she wouldn't be a mother. Her sadness made her calm. After a hysterectomy, for which her mother came to care for her, she grew a little more plump. She was aware that not being able to have children changed the way Tim felt for her, although because this was not her fault, she was also aware that he wanted to be fair toward her. After they made love, he still said thank you, and his thank you was a statement, even a tender statement, of his appreciation of her, however disappointed he was.

In the space of a year, Tim's mother died. Shortly after, his father died, and at his cremation in Golders Green crematorium Tim introduced to Nancy his father's mistress, Helen Phillips, whom he insisted stand by his side. Nancy had not known that Mr. Arbib had a mistress, as Tim did and accepted, and she wondered if Mrs. Arbib had known. Yes, Tim said, she had known, she had known, and that was all he said.

Anxiety always made Tim work, with determination, to put right what was wrong. She knew that he would never give in and accept that wrongs could not be put right, and she admired him for this. And yet she felt pity, if pity was the word, for him, because she knew that his insisting that what was impossibly wrong be put right would not put the wrong right, any more than she could be made to have children for him. She felt tender towards him for what he wanted and what she couldn't give him.

His father's collection of old-master prints was sold at a Christie's auction, with a catalogue devoted to it that reproduced each work, giving its provenance and details of its condition. With his inheritance and the money from the sale, Tim was, after taxes, able to buy a house in upper Hampstead with a white façade and a portico over the black street door. The anxiety of having work done on the house and having it decorated and furnished—the builders never did what they were supposed to in the way Tim wanted it and on time, the decorators' drop cloths didn't cover the parquet floors so paint was splattered on them, the wrong pieces of furniture were delivered—made Tim so agitated that Nancy worried about him.

He assembled his remaining collection—the paintings and brass vessels and glass vials and ancient oil lamps and statuettes—in his new study, propping the smaller paintings against books in the bookshelves where he also placed the objects, and he stacked the larger paintings against a wall. The Torah case he placed on the table in the middle of the study. He kept the door to his study shut, so Nancy glimpsed inside only when he went in or came out and she was nearby. She was aware that this was where he must go for whatever reason he had to withdraw there—to be alone, she thought, and deal with the disorder that made him anxious, and she never entered.

She wanted to allay Tim's anxiety. If she could not make him a father, she could, she thought help him in his professional life. If he was determined, so could she be. When the house was in order, Nancy thought of asking James and Hilary Kess to come for a weekend, and she would give what she had learned to call a drinks party for them. She would ask whom they'd like to have invited, hoping to bring together for Tim a house full of judges.

The Kesses said the weather in the Lowlands had been so bad they hadn't left their kitchen in weeks, except to run, run, through the cold rooms to their bedroom at night to get quickly into bed, and in the morning from bed to the Aga in the kitchen. They'd love to come to London to stay with Nancy and Tim, and it was princely of the young couple to invite them. As for the drinks party, it was royal of them to want to have it. Hilary suggested a few guests, but she must really leave it to them to invite whomever they would like to have. As Nancy didn't know who the right people would be, she left the guest list up to Tim. He made it out carefully, and gave it to her to do the inviting.

"Who is Gabriella Almansi?" Nancy asked.

"An Italian lawyer," Tim answered.

In the early autumn evening, the rooms were becoming dark and Nancy was lighting the lamps when the doorbell rang, and the young woman hired for the party went to open the door for the first guest. A slender woman with a slender neck and short auburn hair and blue eye makeup but no lipstick came in. She was wearing a dark, double-breasted, pin-striped business suit, the skirt narrow and long, with a white blouse, and she went quickly to Nancy to say, with an accent that was like a deep shadow to her clear English, "I am sorry to arrive in my work clothes, but I thought that if I went home to change I would be very late. Now I see I'm early." She held out a slender hand and said, "I am Almansi, Gabriella."

Hilary and James came into the sitting room from upstairs, and Nancy introduced Gabriella to them. James shook her hand, but Hilary, smiling, stood back and, as she had learned to do, fingered her pearl necklace. Gabriella exclaimed to Hilary, "What a very beautiful pearl necklace."

Hilary asked, "Oh, do you like it?" and Gabriella, laughing, said, "Be careful—as a lawyer, I would use all my knowledge to justify my stealing it with impunity." James laughed, and Gabriella turned to him and said, "I think we have common friends." He made her laugh now, asking, "How common?" Nancy and Hilary turned to each other as Gabriella and James talked about their friends in common. An elderly woman came in with a tray of champagne and orange juice.

Tim was not yet down, and Nancy felt awkward introducing herself to other guests who began to arrive. Just as she was about to go upstairs to get Tim, he appeared. She was speaking to three men, trying to keep the conversation about opera at Covent Garden going, and she expected Tim to come to her, but he went immediately to Gabriella and James, who were still talking, she presumed, about their common friends. Hilary, twisting her pearl necklace in her fingers, was standing aside, alone.

Two tall women came in, younger, Nancy thought, than she, and they came to introduce themselves to her with accents Nancy couldn't place. She didn't get their names. In America she would have asked them to repeat their names, but here no one did that, and she continued to try to behave as the English did. Neither could she remember the names of the men, so she stood back a little to make room and, gesturing from one to the other with her arm, let the men introduce themselves. She looked again at Tim talking to Gabriella and James, all of them intent. Tim's neck, she thought, was bulging over his shirt collar.

One of the tall young newcomers was blonde and wore a black cocktail dress with a large rhinestone necklace and long rhinestone earrings. Nancy saw the smooth cleavage between her small breasts. Her shoes had very high heels. The other tall woman was brunette, in a tan silk dress with long sleeves and a high, round neck tied with a bow of the same material.

When Nancy went to Tim to tell him they had come in, he looked over her head and, smiling, said, "They're Brigitte and Erica."

"Who are Brigitte and Erica? Were they on the guest list?" she asked.

He said, "Girls who work in the Temple. I thought I'd ask them. They're German."

"Oh," Nancy said.

Tim said, "I'd better go and talk to them."

After Tim moved away, James left, and Gabriella Almansi was standing alone. By the smile Gabriella gave her, a smile that tried to be open in a face closed with reservations, Nancy knew suddenly that she and Tim were having an affair. She felt a sense of displacement and wondered for an instant who she was and what she was doing at this party in this house, standing in front of this adulterous woman.

She heard herself say, "It was a dreary day, wasn't it?"

Gabriella, who knew exactly who she was and thought she had every reason to be in this house at this party, said, laughing lightly, "You have become very English, talking about the weather." She had, Nancy thought, every right to be having an affair with Tim.

Nancy didn't know what to say to her. As if from a distance, she saw herself introduce Gabriella to a couple standing nearby, and as soon as Gabriella took command of the conversation with them, Nancy, without excusing herself but feeling she had become invisible, turned away from them. She felt that no one at the party, now crowded, saw her.

Involuntarily, she looked again for Gabriella, and saw her talking with another woman.

She didn't go to look for Tim. She went through the guests in the sitting room and the dining room and into the kitchen. The girl who had answered the door was arranging little sausages on a dish. Nancy went past her, through the open back door, and down the cast-iron stairs to the garden. The air in the dark garden was moist and humid, and the thick ivy growing on the back wall looked black. She walked slowly to the end, where there was an old apple tree. Ivy grew up the trunk of the apple tree and about its lower branches. Small creatures moving in it made the ivy rustle abruptly here and there, and then it went still.

Why, she asked herself, hadn't it occurred to her that of course Tim would have an affair? If he had been able to, he would, like his father, have had a mistress, but married men whose fathers had lived in a world in which they had mistresses didn't themselves have mistresses, they had affairs.

She turned round to the back of the house, which was attached to similar houses by shared brick walls, and she saw lighted windows all along. She saw the lighted windows of her kitchen, no one inside, and, above, the lighted windows of the rooms. Hilary stood at one of them, alone, looking out. Nancy drew back, though she was sure Hilary could not see her. Hilary was twisting her necklace in her fingers. Nancy looked up to the lighted windows of what would have been the nursery and saw in one Tim, and in the other the girl with the rhinestone earrings.

She had always thought men were excused for being helpless in what they wanted, but, in her naive egocentricity, she had thought that what men most wanted in their helplessness was support.

Upstairs, Tim gestured to the girl that they must go and opened the door for her to go out first, then shut the door behind him onto the empty room, the light still lit.

Nancy knew he was not doing anything to hurt her. Again she told herself she felt that the very helplessness with which men wanted to make love, the helplessness she thought of, no matter how old and how experienced the man, of a boy wanting to make love for the first time, was their excuse, if they needed an excuse. They didn't. And they shouldn't be blamed for what they longed for. But—, she thought, and she didn't know what she meant by this "but."

In the nursery that Nancy had learned to call the spare room, Hilary turned off the light and disappeared into darkness, then reappeared in the light that shone in from the passage when she opened the door to go back to the party. Nancy wondered about Hilary's withdrawal.

Slowly Nancy returned, because she knew she must, into the house. Tim and the two girls were drinking champagne together on one side of the dining room table, and, without looking at them, Nancy passed on the other side of the table to go into the sitting room.

Gabriella came to her to tell her she must go, and to thank her.

Nancy said, "You were the first to arrive, and you're the first to leave."

Gabriella said, "My husband is waiting at home, and I am sure the baby is howling and he is trying to calm the little darling. You and Tim will come to dinner. I will make you a special Italian Jewish dish."

Nancy felt guilty that she had suspected the sleek and commanding Italian. Taking Gabriella's hand in hers, Nancy, surprised, asked, "You're Jewish?"

"You couldn't tell?"

"I couldn't."

"But Almansi is a Jewish name."

"I didn't know," Nancy said.

"It doesn't matter," Gabriella said, and, still holding Nancy's hand, leaned forward to kiss her on a cheek, and Nancy moved her head so Gabriella kissed her on the lips. Nancy flushed, but Gabriella, stepping back, held Nancy's hand in both hers and said, coolly, "Or perhaps I shall try to cook *alla Americana* for you," and she said goodbye and left Nancy feeling she was an uncultured American.

Tim was coming toward her with the girls on either side of him. He said to Nancy, "Erika has come to thank you before she leaves," and Erika held out her long, thin hand. Tim didn't mention the other girl, who stood behind Erika as Nancy shook Erika's hand and said she was glad she'd had a good time at the party. Erika's small, thin nose was a little crooked at the bridge. Nancy said goodbye to the other girl, and Tim accompanied them out.

Softly clapping his hands, as though he were congratulating himself on a successful performance, James Kess entered the sitting room with Hilary. It had been arranged: they were to have supper out with a judge and his wife.

In what seemed to her a rush, all the guests approached Nancy to thank her and say goodbye, and she, a little detached, tried her best to make them think she was happier that they had come than that they were leaving. They were all gone within ten minutes.

Tim said to Nancy, "I'm going into the kitchen for grub."

"I'll get you something to eat," she said.

In the kitchen, while the helpers quietly cleaned up, Tim sat at one end of the kitchen table with a plate of cold chicken and salad and a bottle of champagne, and Nancy, who wasn't eating or drinking, sat at the other end.

Tired, she put her elbows on the edge of the table and held her head up, her hands under her jaw. She watched Tim eat and drink. His taut neck muscles swelled against his stiff, white, shiny collar, which, because his shirt was striped, looked like an old-fashioned detachable collar. His lips were thin, as were his nostrils and the lobes of his ears. His hair, with a rigidly straight parting that showed his white skull, was combed smoothly in place. It was, she thought, a sort of groomed starkness.

The helpers finished their work and stood by the table while Tim, leaning back in his chair, reached into the inside pocket of his suit jacket for his wallet, extracted some bills, and held them out to the older woman who, it seemed to Nancy, curtsied just a little as she took them. He said, "You'll sort out between you who is owed what. And, mind, I don't want one of you suing the other and coming to me for legal aid."

The two laughed and left, only turning back at the door to say goodnight to Nancy.

Nancy said to Tim, "During the party, I went out into the back garden."

He poured himself another glass of champagne. "To get away for a bit? I don't blame you. I hate parties as well as anyone, but, here we are, they are useful. And, I must say, darling, on the whole it was quite a useful party. Thank you for your pains."

She said, "From outside, I saw the light on in what was meant to be the nursery."

Tim thrust out his jaw, apparently thinking. "As evidence of what, do you think?"

"I saw you and the German girl in the room."

"And what were we doing?"

"Talking."

"Quite right. We were talking. She is a Cambridge graduate, speaks not only German and English and French and Italian and Spanish, but also Russian. Do you know the Russian word for kiss is something like *pazzo-lui*, which in Italian means he's crazy?"

"I did know."

"I was proposing to Erika that she work for me."

"I'm sure, with all her languages, she'll be very useful, in the new, united, multilingual Europe and all that. Is she Jewish?"

"Does she, do you think, have a Jewish name?"

"I'm sort of vague about what is and what isn't a Jewish name."

"She doesn't, but, yes, her mother is Jewish."

"It doesn't matter," Nancy said.

Tim drank down the champagne, then, with the tips of

his fingers, he pushed the glass a full arm's length away on the table. "I shall now do a little reading of certain papers for tomorrow."

That "certain" meant the papers were important, and also meant she should ask him about these important papers. He had always counted on her interest, and he counted on it now, to listen to him talk about his work. She said, "Tell me," as tears rose into her eyes.

He said, "You're tired. Go to bed, darling. I'll stay up to read, but won't be late coming to bed myself."

"You're sure you don't want to talk?"

"Thank you, but I'll be able to sort everything out, this one time, without having to talk it through with you. Go to bed."

He was tender in his consideration for her, and his tenderness made the tears rise more and run down the sides of her nose.

Tim got up and stood over her. "You're weeping."

As she looked up at him, blinking, tears ran down her face.

"I know how demanding I can be," he said, "and I must tell you I am sorry."

"I don't mind your being demanding," she said. "It's just that—"

"What?"

"I don't know if I'll be able to do enough."

"You find I am demanding more than you can give?"

"Sometimes."

He looked away from her.

She said, "I thought it'd be enough, helping you as much as I could by supporting you in your world."

Looking down at her again, he said, "But you've already proven yourself in that, which is more than enough for me."

A small sob broke from her and she pressed her hand to her mouth. Tim leaned forward and kissed the top of her head. Weeping, Nancy asked, "Why did you marry me? I'm not beautiful, I'm not rich, as an American. I'm no help to you here. And now I can't have your child. Why?"

This made Tim stand back. He asked, "Don't you know?"

"No, no."

"I married you because I loved you, though I once did tell you I don't use the word love."

Pressing both hands to her mouth, Nancy rose and hurried out.

In bed, when, finally, she heard Tim come into the room, she pretended to be asleep. From what seemed a great remove from him, she heard him undress and carefully hang his clothes up and put on his pajamas and come to the bed, and as he got into bed her sense of removal became greater.

They lay side by side, and Nancy imagined that all about them was a big hollow, and the bed floated in that hollow.

Surprise jolted her body when she heard, just heard before she understood, Tim say, "Have you been having suspicions about me?"

The hollow they were in expanded so much their bed became, in it, tiny, and her voice, which surprised her when she heard it as much as Tim's had, was also tiny. She said, "Yes."

"Ah."

"Do I have reason to feel suspicious?"

The hollow expanded more, and Tim said, "Yes, you do." He turned toward her and asked, "Shall I tell you about it now?"

"Is it Erika?"

"It's Erika."

"Why did you lie?"

"I did not lie. I do want her to work for me. What I didn't tell you is that I've made her pregnant."

"She didn't look pregnant. She looked skinny."

"That is as is."

"And she'll have the baby?"

"I want her to have it."

"And you'll want to marry her?"

"I won't want to marry her. I will, however, set her up in a flat with the child and, from time to time, stay with them."

"And you'll go on being married and, whenever you're not there, living with me?"

"If you accept that."

"And if I don't?"

"The choice you have is between that and filing for divorce, which I would have no reason to contest. This may make my chances for becoming a judge difficult, but I won't give up my child. And because I won't give up my child, and because the child is Erika's as well, I have to establish a separate household for the child and her."

"And if I divorce you?"

"I would not marry Erika."

"And if she wants to marry someone else?"

"The child is mine."

"You've both agreed to that?"

"We have."

"She sounds practical."

"She is."

"And you sound practical, too."

"Jews tend to be practical."

"Do they?"

"In my experience of Jews."

"You would like me to accept all this?"

"Yes, I would like you to. But please do not think I demand it of you. You must think about it and tell me, in your own time, what you conclude."

"I wish I had your power of analysis. I really admire the way you can analyze a situation and reach a conclusion about it."

"Thank you," he said. "But this is about feeling. We once talked of feelings, feelings too vast to be named. I told you how much I want a child. How much I want children. Can that desire have a name? It's immense. It's the closest I shall ever get to an immortal need—no, to a mortal need. A marriage without a child, however close, however loving, is to me like a suicide pact, the closeness, the loving, end in death, no more. There is something deadly in a marriage without children. Yes, deadly."

She closed her eyes as if to take all this in as feeling, and she did, she did enough to open her eyes and say, "We could adopt."

"You know me well enough, you've suffered me enough, to know the child must be mine. Forgive me, darling, forgive me, as I once told you I would need forgiveness, but our marriage is dead to me. This is not your fault. I assure you, I do not in any way think this is your fault. You can't help yourself. But neither can I help myself. I can't die without having a child to keep me alive in this world, this so terribly, terribly, terribly destructive world, a world that has wanted the end of me and my line. I refuse to give in to the destruction. I refuse. I can't die without having a child to keep me and my line alive in this destructive world. I refuse to die out, to be made to die out. They want us dead, they want us dead, but I won't die. I will stay alive in a son."

"A son?"

"A son, yes, yes, a son. There, you have the full blast of my ego. A son, a magnificently masculine son who will have sons, who will have sons, who will have sons. Do you at all understand this need?"

"No." She lay still. She said, quietly, "I feel, instead, that I want to die."

"You admit this finally. I have always sensed that in you. You've repressed it, you've repressed it very well, admirably well, but you've been defeated."

"Yes," Nancy agreed weakly.

"What defeated you? Did I?"

"Yes, you." She again lay still. "No," she said, "not you. I don't know what defeated me."

"But you won't die."

"No, I won't die."

"I couldn't bear that, darling. That would break me. Though I can hardly bring myself to give it a name, you at one time recognized grief in me, the blame caused by grief. If that was all the expression of grief I was capable of, it was almost more than I could bear. I couldn't bear more blame. You understand that, don't you?"

"I understand. I understand because I have never stopped

feeling blame for someone whose life I think I destroyed."

"You've told me."

"I've not told you, not really. I've repressed that, too. I left him when he most needed me, and I'm sure that destroyed him. And I'm to blame."

Tim's voice too went quiet. He said, "Do we exaggerate our sense of blame because we feel, all of us, that we were, that we are, to blame for the mass destruction forced on us? That we were, that we are, to blame for the world wanting us dead? Why, at some deep level, do we think we are to blame?"

"I don't know, Tim. I don't know anything."

"You can say the same about me."

"You know a lot."

"I know nothing, but in my ignorance I am determined to force myself on the world."

Her mind went out, far, to the edge of the vast, still hollow, from where she looked back at them both.

She asked in a dry whisper, "What did you mean when you once said your wife was an American mystic?"

He placed the back of his hand on his forehead. "As far as I sensed, which was not far, for I only had a sense of what she believed, which she kept from me—when she would withdraw into herself—or perhaps she didn't withdraw, but, instead, expanded far outside herself, out into the views that seemed to be so meaningful to her, that became more and more meaningful to her the more ill she became—I sensed her need for more than I or anyone could give her, her need for, oh, everything, as if everything could be had. She wanted everything, I felt, everything all together. If she was Jewish, she was Jewish American, and she was vastly more American than she was Jewish. Sometimes I thought she was not at all Jewish."

"And you, a Jew, thought what she believed nonsense."

He dropped his hand to his chest. "It is nonsense, but I never told her so. She believed her death must have meaning in the ultimate union with everything, and I swear I never disabused her of the idea. Never. She died believing in the vast ultimate that her death had meaning. But death has no meaning, none. Destruction has no meaning, none. Suffering has no meaning, none. There is no meaning to life either, but we must live."

"And you are determined to live."

"I am."

A sudden arousal in Nancy made her draw her hair back from her face and hold it together at her nape, and her voice, as of itself, rose. "But your life is all pretension."

He raised a hand, as if to guard himself.

She lowered her voice and said, "I'm not condemning you. You need your pretensions, and, yes, I understand the need. Build on your pretensions, build and build and build, and maybe you'll finally convince yourself that you're no longer pretending, but are the real right thing. But you'll never be the real right thing. Never. I wish that for you, I do, but you'll never be the real right thing."

He lowered his arm. "You're right. And I know I'll never convince myself I'm the real right thing. But, believe me, I'm not pretending when I say I want a son."

"A Jewish son."

"A Jewish son."

"I would have loved to give you a Jewish son."

He cried, "Oh my darling."

She turned away from him.

"Do you forgive me?" he asked.

Her back to him, she laughed lightly and said, "I forgive you."

He didn't laugh. "Thank you."

Nancy remained out at the far edge and didn't sleep all night; her eyes remained open as if she were far out in space and looking back at the world, and as if it were looking back at the world that made her eyes fill up with tears. She didn't move when, at dawn, Tim got up. She stayed in bed while he was out of the room. She, too, should get up and make sure their guests had breakfast, but she would let Tim do that. He came back into the room to dress, and she turned over to lie with her face in the pillow. The bedroom door closed, and she shifted onto her back and opened her eyes. She lay for a while longer.

The house was quiet when she got up. In her dressing gown she went downstairs and, on impulse, to the door to Tim's study, and she leaned against it to listen for any movement inside, thinking he might be there. She dared herself to open the door as slowly and noiselessly as possible, to make her entrance unobtrusive even into a room with no one else present. The shutters on the window were closed, so the room was dim. She opened the shutters, and as she turned back into the room the Torah case drew her attention shining in the morning light beaming through the window. She approached the case carefully, as always to be unobtrusive, and she studied the case. She hadn't noticed before that in places it was dented, in places the silver embossing worn. She touched a little gold bell, which gave off a faint, resonant clink. What, she asked herself, what did this mean to Tim? For her a resonating object, resonant of a religion constantly under scrutiny from outside, constantly debased from outside, constantly open to destruction from outside? She would never have been able to ask Tim the question; he already knew the answer. She ran a finger around the bells hanging on one of the elaborate globes, to make the gold bells ring together, a delicate carillon.

The guests had gone.

Deep in bath foam, she watched the rain hit the window. As she was putting on her robe, her body still a little moist, she was sure she heard someone walking downstairs, and she knew it couldn't be Tim, who was out. Her scalp tight and tingling, Nancy did something that she knew was absurd, but she did it before her awareness of its absurdity could stop her: she picked up a bottle of cologne from a shelf, uncapped it, and poured some between her breasts, and as she went out of the bathroom and through her bedroom to the passage, she smeared the scent on her neck and her breasts and under her arms.

She stood at the top of the narrow stairs, listening. Hearing nothing for a long while but the beating of her pulse, she thought she had only imagined footsteps, and she turned away, then stopped, stark still, when the footsteps sounded from below, more and more faint as they went from one room to another. The footsteps stopped, and she descended the stairs, often pausing, one hand on the rail and the other holding her dressing gown closed over her breasts, to listen. At the bottom of the staircase she again stood still; then, as if suddenly and helplessly pulled forward by her fear, she went barefoot along the passage to the archway into the sitting room, which was filled with rain light that made the room appear empty. She went through the room into the dining room, her breathing as quick as her pulse. The dining room, too, was completely empty, and she rushed through it, excited, to open the door to the kitchen. No one was there.

Back in her room, she quickly dressed and went out, not quite knowing where she was going. All of London became a thin, moving cloud, with the pale white and red lights of cars appearing and disappearing in it. On Park Road, across from the mosque in Regent's Park, she saw, ahead of her in the mist, a man, alone, waiting at a bus stop, and all at once she was sure that the man was Yvon Gendreau. She did not know if she should hurry on to him or draw back, and as she stared at him a double-decker bus came along and stopped by him, and he boarded. The bus was lit up inside. It passed her and she looked through the wide windows for him, but she saw only an old woman sitting toward the back.

four

From a window in the living room of her parents' apartment, Nancy looked out at the autumnal trees in Central Park. When she turned back to the living room, she saw her mother standing in the dim light.

Nancy said, "You came in so quietly, I didn't hear you."

"You used to say that often when you'd turn around and see me standing in a room," her mother said.

"Did I?"

"You don't remember?"

Nancy smiled.

Her mother came to her and, taking Nancy by an arm, slowly drew her toward the light through the window, then drew away from her daughter and looked out the window and said, "Look, how the trees have become autumnal. I hadn't noticed."

Mother and daughter stood side by side at the window.

"Are you sure you don't want to see Dr. Quinn?" Nancy's mother said to her. "He's known you since you were a little girl."

"All I need is to be calm for a while."

"I understand."

Wind blew against the window, then blew out over Central Park.

Nancy asked, "Jews are not supposed to be concerned about an afterlife and all that, isn't that so?"

"If you tell me it's so."

"Do you ever think of an afterlife?"

"If it's Jewish not to, I guess I'm Jewish because, no, I don't think about it."

"And you don't think of death?"

"I try not to."

"You're not frightened of death?"

Her mother said in her low, expressionless voice, "No."

A burst of cold wind hurled itself against the glass trying to get in.

"You won't call any of your old friends?" her mother asked.

"Not yet."

On her way through the living room, she noted the Biedermeier furniture and, especially, on the mantelpiece one of the Berlin porcelain ice pails.

Her mother followed her, as if neither she nor Nancy knew why, and she stopped when Nancy stopped by the mantel to examine the figures of a diminutive couple walking away along a narrow road.

"Everything from Germany," Nancy said.

And her mother said, softly, "From a Germany that no longer exists," and left her, and Nancy felt very alone.

She remembered this: when she was young and in school she met the parents of friends who seemed to her more

American than her own parents, her parents more and more foreign to her as she, at school and parties and out on dates, became more and more American. Even when she found out that her friends and the parents of her friends were Jewish, they seemed more American than Jewish. Nancy was once invited to a Sabbath dinner where white candles were lit and her school friend and his father wore skullcaps, and she thought that the Jews around the table were American Jews, and that her parents were not, but were German Jews. And as she grew up in America, it seemed to Nancy that, if she at odd moments did think, yes, her parents were Jewish, and, after all, had had to escape Germany for their lives, and had had relatives who weren't able to escape, they were German Jews, were displaced German Jews, who would want displaced German furniture. And this made Nancy even lonelier for her lonely parents.

She thought of Aaron, Aaron Cohen, about whom she knew nothing but that he was the most displaced Jew she had ever met.

She dressed to go out, but before leaving she looked for her mother, whom she found sitting alone in the armchair she usually sat in for after-dinner coffee in her husband's office, as if this was the place where she could be most private, and Nancy said, "I thought I'd go for a walk," and her mother smiled and hoped she'd keep warm because there was a cold wind outside.

She went out into the cold wind in Central Park.

She would go to where Aaron Cohen had lived, and the wind seemed to impel her on her way across the park to the West Side and along Eighty-Ninth Street to where, her wide-brimmed hat and trailing scarf pulled by the wind, she climbed the steps to the stoop and rang the bell she remembered to Aaron's room, and when she did she felt that she shouldn't have come, that she must leave before anyone could answer. And she asked herself why had she come, because Aaron wouldn't be there, Aaron would be somewhere else that she couldn't imagine.

But Aaron appeared. He was more gaunt than she remembered, but, as in the past, he was wearing a sweatshirt and plain chinos.

He smiled and she laughed because she didn't know what to say.

She thought she would leave when another gust of wind pulled at her and she said, "I suppose I can't come up to your room because you're a monk now."

Smiling still, he said, "I'm sorry but, you're right, it's against my vows for you to come up to my room."

"Vinnie would say you've become a real Catholic."

"There's more to it than Vinnie used to think."

"Do you see him?"

"I do, sometimes for a walk along Riverside Park."

"And what do you talk about?"

"About how unhappy he is."

"And do you help him to be happy?"

"I try."

She asked, "Can I at least come in out of the wind?"

"I should have asked you to," he said, and opened the door wider for her to step into the entrance hall.

Nancy asked, "And how are the cows and pigs and sheep?"

"They're pretty good, thanks."

She turned away, as though to leave, but she turned back and asked, "Why did you become a monk? Can I just ask you that?"

"You can."

"Tell me. I need to know. And then I'll leave you, because I know you want me to leave."

"No, I don't want you to leave, but even if you stayed I don't know if I could answer your question."

"Try. Try for me."

He leaned his head to the side and said, as if as an aside, "To pray."

"To pray for what?" she asked.

"For you."

She felt a little heave in her breath, but before she could speak a light was switched on in the entrance hall and the stairway, and someone was descending the stairs; he was wearing what she thought was a monk's robe but with a padded coat over it. Aaron introduced Nancy to him, and she heard him call Aaron Damian. Something gave way in Nancy that weakened her, and she thought there was nothing for her here, nothing, and though the other monk, whose name she had already forgotten, was with Aaron, she said goodbye to him but not to the other monk, and quickly went down the steps to the pavement, from which she looked back at the two monks in the light of the entrance hall. She raised a hand and they both raised hands to her, then the door closed.

She felt too weak to walk and hailed a taxi whose headlights were beaming palely in the dusk.

* * *

She thought, on an impulse that needed no thinking about, she would go to Boston to find Yvon.

That evening at dinner, cooked by her mother and served by Nancy, her father said to her, "I don't know why, but I never thought it'd work between you and Tim."

"Because we're so different?"

"You could say that."

Before she went to bed, Nancy went into her parents' bedroom, where they sat propped up in bed, her mother reading a novel and her father a news magazine. Going from one side of the bed to the other, she kissed them good night.

"I've decided to go to Boston," she said.

Her mother said, "Stay with us for a while, don't hurry away."

"We'd like you to stay," her father said.

She stayed until autumn evolved into winter, and day after day she spent with her parents, to whom she thought she had never felt so close, and they to her, as if a deep sense of the unspoken had opened up between her and them. Not since she was a girl had she been out shopping with her mother, and she found herself as indecisive as her mother about a winter coat, and finally let her mother decide. And winter snow began.

As she drove to Boston, the awareness of difference caused by becoming used to cars driving on the other side of the road startled her when, for a second, she thought she was on the wrong side and felt she was both back in her country and outside it. The feeling deepened on the interstate highway, and she told herself she had driven this route over and over so had no reason to imagine she had never driven it before. Passing the waterworks with water fountaining in round pools, the electrical power installation behind a chain-link fence, the cinder-block warehouse covered with fading, spray-can graffiti, she thought she was experiencing déjà vu, and that she of course had seen these many times before in exactly the places where they were now.

Large blackbirds settled on the snow-white verges along either side of the highway only to fly off again. Stopping for coffee or lunch, or passing the wide green exit signs off the highway into Providence, she had the same sensation of knowing she had been in the place before but of not being able to remember when, and the sensation became overwhelming as she drove over highways toward what looked, at a distance, to be snow-bound Boston.

She parked her car in an underground parking garage and walked up to the Common where, it seemed to her, she noticed things she had never noticed when she lived in Boston: chains strung from pole to pole along the paths, lamps, benches, and she wondered how she could not remember ever having seen the monument to the Civil War, everything heaped with snow. She walked up to the snow-filled Frog Pond and farther up, to Beacon Street, and from Beacon Street farther up onto Beacon Hill.

And here everything became so familiar and so different she was not sure if she was there or not. As she approached the street, down the other side of the Hill, on which she had lived with Yvon and where he might for all she knew still be living, she felt an inward impulse both to draw away and to go to the street door and ring the bell. The brick sidewalk had been shoveled, and there was a bank of snow along the curb in which the posts of the gas streetlights were partly buried. She looked up at the streetlight that had illuminated the room where she and Yvon had made love and talked and slept. Lit all day, the pale greenish flames in the glass lanterns hissed. She climbed the three granite steps to the newly painted black door with a newly polished brass knocker; to the side of the door were brass slots for the names and bells of the occupants. The one where her name had been was empty.

She rang the bell. She waited. There was no answer. It was early afternoon. If Yvon were teaching at the language school, he would be there, and would return.

In a telephone booth deep in a bank of snow she telephoned information for the number of the family home of Manos Papas, then telephoned there, and Manos's mother answered. She remembered Nancy and asked how she was, but said quickly, with an accent Nancy didn't remember, that Manos was an intern now, with a Greek wife and a baby. She gave Nancy his telephone number. Through the glass sides of the telephone booth, she looked out at people passing along the narrow path through the snowbank on the sidewalk. She was not sure the number she dialed was right. The palms of her hands sweated as she waited for the ringing telephone to be answered, and they sweated more when a woman answered. Nancy explained, tactfully implying she had no other interest in Manos, past or present or future, but to find out something through him, that she was trying to locate an old friend of theirs, Yvon Gendreau. Manos's wife said, Oh hi, her name was Irini, and Manos had spoken about her and would want to see her.

"Where are you staying in Boston?" Irini asked.

Nancy hadn't thought about where she would stay. She said, because she remembered it was the hotel where students from colleges outside of Boston stayed when they came for proms or football games, "The Kenilworth."

"Can you come to dinner tonight?" Irini asked. "It'll be a nice surprise for Manos when he gets home."

"I can," Nancy answered.

She walked back toward the Public Garden and the Ritz, where she got a room for the night, and from her room she watched the day go dark and the lights light in the Public Garden and, beyond, on the Common, illuminating the snow-covered landscape where there was no one, and where, no doubt, it was dangerous to go at night.

Manos and Irini lived in Brookline in a new apartment house. Manos opened the door to Nancy and hugged but didn't kiss her. Irini, who had blonde hair and blue eyes, stood down the entry hall from Manos.

Releasing Manos, Nancy immediately said to him, because she couldn't help herself, "Please tell me about Yvon."

"I'll tell you," Manos said.

"Come in," Irini said to Nancy, "come in."

Manos helped Nancy off with her coat.

She tried to check her compulsion to talk about Yvon during drinks and dinner, which Irini served at a long, shining table with candles in silver candlesticks at either end, and even for a while after dinner, while Irini told Nancy about how she and Manos had met, about their Greek Orthodox wedding, about the baby, asleep, and about Manos wanting to become a heart specialist. Manos smiled while Irini spoke.

They moved to the living room. Irini stopped talking for a while, then got up and said, "I'll let you two continue," and said good night and left.

Looking around, Nancy noticed that there was nothing Greek about the apartment, not even a rug. With one corner of her lips raised, Nancy said, "You married a Greek."

He laughed as if at a joke he had made. "It pleased my parents."

And she laughed at the joke.

Surprising her because she'd never known him to be concerned. Manos said, "This country has changed in the time you've been away, Nan. It was always uncontrollable, and that was a great virtue, because the uncontrollable allowed for freedom. But it's become so uncontrollable I'm frightened for my family. The fear is real. I wonder what's going to come out of the chaos, and I don't know and I don't know anyone who does. What's strange is that the chaos seems to make people more patriotic than ever."

She asked, "Where is Yvon?"

"I can't say quite where."

"You can't say to *me*?"

"Nan, he was really broken after you left him."

"I had to leave him. It was either him or me. And I'm not going to feel guilty that I broke him. He almost broke me."

"Then why have you come back to look for him?"

She lowered her head, then, raising it, said, "Because I want to see him."

"In fact, I can't say because he told me he was leaving Boston, but he didn't say where he was going."

"Back to his parish, I'll bet."

"I hope not. I hope he went somewhere where he started a new life."

Nancy asked, "Will you get my coat for me?"

In her hotel room in the Ritz, she opened the curtains, which the maid had closed, on the view of the Public Garden and Common and went to bed with them open.

She did not want to go to Providence, and even while she was in her car heading south she kept telling herself to drive past and go on back to New York. But she turned off at the exit.

In downtown Providence, she got out of her car to walk around to calm herself and then, in the city's main post office, looked up in the Yellow Pages, under Printing Businesses, the name Gendreau. She asked a policeman sitting in his car near where her car was parked for directions to the address she had written with an eyebrow pencil on the back of an envelope. He took a plan of the city and its suburbs from his glove compartment to look it up.

"That's in the French parish," he said.

"I know," she said. "I've been there before, but I can't remember how to get there. It seems a long way away."

"I'd say, centuries away."

She drove up a hill out of the city, past churches, all red brick, that looked the same to her. Unsure of herself, she stopped before a church to ask an old woman walking along the sidewalk with two big sagging bags of grocery shopping if this was the French parish, and the old woman said, no, it was the Polish parish, though, she added, there were not many Poles left to make it a parish. The French parish was at the top of the hill.

Nancy parked her car in a side street next to the brick church at the top of the hill. She got out and walked along the path on the sidewalk between the snowbank at the curb and the snowbank against the wooden and chain-link fences of the front yards of tenement houses; great icicles hung from their eaves. At the end of a row of shops she came to a snow-covered lot, dry weeds growing up through the snow, and she saw GENDREAU PRINTING across the large window of a shop there. Through the large window, partly frosted over, she saw a man she imagined must be Yvon's brother Cyriac at the press. Just as she was thinking she shouldn't have come, he turned and saw her.

He opened the door, an old-fashioned door with a glass pane in it and a half-drawn blind with a cord and a wooden knob at the end of the cord that hit against the glass, and he rushed out onto the path, but stopped a short distance from her, as if he didn't know how to greet her. Their breaths steamed in the cold air. He looked like a rough Yvon.

"You're cold," he said.

She said, "I'm an old friend of Yvon, Nancy Green."

"Ah, Nancy," he said, matter-of-factly. "Come in, come in," he said, and tightened an arm about her shoulders to bring her inside the printing shop.

The press was clanking. He shut it off.

"You shouldn't have done that," she said.

"It's fine. I can come back. I have time."

He was standing at the large press, rubbing his hands together to try to get the ink off them.

"What were you printing?" she asked.

He hesitated and then said, "Some fliers for the liquor store. They're having a sale."

"In French?"

"In English. The owner of the liquor store is Irish now."

Nancy asked, "Is Yvon here in the parish?"

Cyriac laughed. "The parish? The parish doesn't exist anymore." And before she could say anything more, he asked, "Did you eat?"

"No," she answered.

"We'll go to my house and eat."

They walked along the parish streets, under the huge, snow-heavy maple trees along the curbs, to the clapboard bungalow that Nancy remembered and that had the familiar smell of wood smoke. Its kitchen walls seemed to converge on the large, black-framed oleograph of Christ holding his chest open to a thorn-entangled heart.

Nancy said, "There used to be an old cabinet in the kitchen. You could see the marks of the adze on the wood."

He said, "I sold it."

"Yvon was proud of it. It had so much history in it."

"So much history, so much," he said, "and it's gone."

As polite as Yvon, Cyriac helped Nancy off with her coat and hung it, with his, in the closet in which she remembered seeing a sheep's pelt, and it was still there.

She followed him into a pantry off the kitchen where, at a sink, Cyriac washed his hands with a paste he scooped out of a can. Ink remained under his nails and in the whorls of the tips of his fingers. From a pantry cabinet he took down a can of food and, holding it out to her, said, "Franco-American spaghetti," and laughed. "The only sign of anything Franco-American in America, and it isn't Franco." He took a loaf of sliced white bread from a tin bread bin. Cyriac, setting the table, put the knives and forks together at one side of the plate, and Nancy recalled Yvon's doubt about what side the knife was set on and what side the fork, and this recollection seemed for a moment to sum up his world. Nancy and Cyriac ate the spaghetti in a thin tomato sauce from mismatched plates and drank tea from mismatched cups without saucers.

Nancy said, "Tell me where Yvon is."

Cyriac seemed to smile a little. "Well, I believe Yvon is gone."

All the tendons of her body became loose, and, as if giving in to something she could no longer hold away, Nancy sat back in her chair. She felt a tingling about her lips.

Nancy asked, "What do you mean, 'you believe'?"

Cyriac said, "I believe," and paused, and Nancy wondered for a flash if he wouldn't tell her, but when he spoke he spoke simply, "that he went into the forest and didn't come out."

She winced. "I don't understand."

"Well, Yvon usually didn't tell me where he went, and I didn't ask. He'd go off for longer and longer times, across the country, maybe without knowing where he was going, maybe just hitching rides. I guess he found jobs, odd jobs, for money enough. But he always came back afterward, sometimes months later, with another piece of rock from where he'd gone. But this time he never returned. And so I think that when the snow was falling heavy, he went into the forest and he found a deep drift, and he laid himself down in the drift, and he fell asleep."

Cyriac ceased talking, as if he had no more to say, and Nancy looked around the kitchen. The worn linoleum patterned with merry-go-rounds and clowns still covered the floor.

"You're a New Yorker, aren't you?" Cyriac asked.

"I am."

"I don't have a problem with New Yorkers. They're buying houses in the woods in the Yankee southern part of the state. They go for walks in the woods, but the Yankees hunt. I sometimes feel that Yvon went there, but if he was there, he'd of been found."

"Did you contact the police?"

"I did, and once or twice they called me to come identify a body, but it wasn't Yvon."

"And did you go to look, yourself?"

"I did, I looked, but he's gone, Nancy, yes, oh yes, he's gone."

"Yes," Nancy repeated quietly.

"Eat up," Cyriac said, and in a state of numbness she did as she was told, with bread.

When she had finished, Nancy said, as if this were the inevitable reaction to not knowing where Yvon was, "Show me the parish."

"I told you, the parish hardly exists anymore."

"Show me what's left."

Nothing of what she remembered the parish to have been was the parish in fact—small, clapboard bungalows behind snow-covered privet hedges; then, as they walked in silence towards the brick bell tower of a church, clapboard tenements with sagging porches at every story, some of the porches with clotheslines strung between pillars and hung with clothes frozen in the cold. There were shops that appeared to be shut, but pale light showed through their frosted windows: a grocery, a laundry, a cobbler's shop. The brick church appeared on a little rise among the tenements and shops. While Nancy waited outside the closed doors of the church, Cyriac went to the rectory for the key to the side door. She felt that she was surrounded by what she could only think of as an inevitability, as though inevitability were a space around her, and in that space was Yvon's world, and his world now was more vast than she could know. Cyriac returned with the key and led her to a side door, which he held open for her to go in first.

The church was colder inside than the outside. The altar, behind a wooden rail, looked stark, a lamp suspended by chains, a tiny red light seeming to flicker in it, hanging above the altar.

She asked, pointing to above the altar where there was what looked like a very small chapel in white and gilt, and she asked, "Is that a tabernacle?"

"How did you know?"

"Yvon told me. He told me it's a bad swearword in your French when you're angry, and that makes me think that I never heard him use any swearwords because I never saw him angry."

"No, not Yvon," his brother said.

"So this is where Yvon came to Mass," Nancy said.

"This is it."

"Tell me, did he believe?"

"Maybe yes, maybe no. It don't matter, not now. Almost no one comes to Mass. And there are no baptisms, so I don't even know where the baptismal fount is, if it's anywheres."

Sunlight lit the stained-glass windows, and she noted that along the bottom of the windows, were painted, in script, French names—Francoeur, Pelletier, Beauchemin—and Cyriac explained that these were the names of the parishioners who had donated the windows; before she could ask, he added that the Gendreaus were never rich enough to donate. There was a hole in one of the windows, as though a stone had been thrown through.

Nancy tried to imagine Yvon sitting in a pew in the church, and she could only see him alone, with no one else and no service at the altar. She thought that if there had been a God present in this church, that God would have been for Yvon alone, as strange to the outside as a God to whom prayers were unknown, but known by Yvon, and, perhaps, still known by him.

"Let's go," Nancy said.

Outside, the sky had clouded over with low gray clouds.

This was what Nancy felt: she felt, yes, that the world was vast, more vast than she could know, than anyone could know.

Cyriac said, "We'll get back into the kitchen, the only room that's warm in the house."

Inside, in the fug of the kitchen, she sat at the table and

he put a battered kettle on the hob, mugs and a bottle of milk and a sugar bowl with a spoon on the table, and while they waited for the water to boil she looked at the large, black-framed oleograph of Christ holding his chest open to a thorn-entangled heart, the picture high on the wall in the absence of the cabinet.

All of Cyriac's attention seemed to be on preparing her a mug of tea: how much milk? how much sugar? She said just tea. He seemed not to know that people drank tea without milk and sugar. His tea was almost half milk and three tea-spoons of sugar.

He said, "You know, Yvon had this idea of finding a new mineral that'd make his collection special, even, well, you'd say unique. He was crazy about his rock collection."

"Do you have his rock collection? Can I see it?"

"I'll show it to you."

"Now."

"Drink your tea."

She drank some tea.

Cyriac said, "He had his ideas, Yvon did, and sometimes they were big ideas, like having all the different rocks from all over the world in his collection. I don't know what it's like to have ideas like that, but I wanted him, wanted Yvon, to do everything he wanted to do, and to get everything he wanted. It was so much that he wanted. Oh, I don't mean getting rich, getting famous, having what a Yankee has, no, that wasn't what Yvon wanted, and I can guess that he didn't want all of that because he knew he couldn't have it, but it was like something bigger than anybody can have."

Nancy heard herself moan a little. "Oh yes."

"You know?"

"I know."

"And you understand?"

"I understand."

"He had it in him that he could make people feel there was something more in the world for them than they knew. He could do that, yes, oh yes, sure, he could make people think there was something more in rocks than just rocks, something they never thought was worth looking at, like rocks. Yvon was the only one who could make Ma be calm, the way she'd be calm at Mass with him sitting next to her. And that's why he came back every weekend to take her to Mass, because she was calm there with him. Just putting his hand on hers when she was hitting her knuckles against the edge of the table, that made her calm. She could be crazy, Ma could, and only Yvon gave her peace, not much, but some. He could do that, Yvon could, he could make her feel that there was something more than just herself, something that would make her let go and be calm, a little, so she'd stop hitting her knuckles on the table and she'd sit back and close her eyes, and he'd sit with her, and maybe he'd close his eyes, too."

Cyriac asked Nancy if she'd like more tea, but she shook her head.

He said, "When we were growing up, Yvon and me, I'd look at the two of them, Ma and Yvon, and I remember when he'd come in and he'd say to Ma, look, look, Ma, look what I found, and he'd show her a piece of rock, maybe quartz, and Ma would try to show him she was as full of wonder about the rock as he was. She would say, It's like it fell from heaven, so you know there's some poetry in Francos. But I'd feel so bad that she'd put such will into showing him how wonderful the rock was. Ma lived on her will, if, that is, she had much of a will to live."

Cyriac rose a little, as if about to get up for something to show her, then he sat back at the table and laughed a light laugh that, maybe, was behind all his talk.

"I couldn't do that for Ma, show her anything that she'd say was wonderful, because I knew that even if she tried nothing was wonderful for Ma. That was the way she was, and I didn't mind, not at all, lucky for me that nothing was expected of me by Ma, except, I knew, that I'd be the one to stay home and take care of her. I didn't expect anything from Ma. Not me. I left high school when I was sixteen, and then I was an apprentice to the printer who had the press, my uncle, the brother of my father. Yvon and me, we were still boys when our father died. We were living with Ma, we'd see her at her crazy times, walking from room to room, hitting the door jambs. And if I remember anything from when my father was alive, it was him telling her, in French, that she was a condemned woman, and why did he marry a condemned woman?"

As if alerted, Nancy asked, "Condemned?"

But, again, Cyriac laughed his light laugh.

"Well, that's what I remember. Yvon, he remembered different, he remembered Pa saying to her, 'Look on the bright side, use your will to look on the bright side.' I'm different than Yvon, I look on the darker side, and I accept that. But Yvon, he couldn't accept that, and he was always trying to get out to where everything would be bright. And sometimes it looked like he was out there, where everything was bright and, yes, wonderful. She knew, Ma knew, she was on the deepest dark side, and she wanted Yvon out, and it was only when he was really out that she could feel happy for him. I understood Ma, I think I understood her more than Yvon, who didn't really understand much, not, really, about anything. You'll laugh, but that's the truth about Yvon."

Nancy smiled. "I know what you mean."

"Anyway, Yvon knew he couldn't blame Ma for what she was, because she couldn't help herself, she didn't have the will. You see, Ma was, well, a kind of innocent, it was beyond her all that made her helpless, and, I'll tell you, I loved Ma for her helplessness. And, here's something else I'll tell you, I loved my brother Yvon for his helplessness, that made him, too, a kind of innocent. He tried and he tried, but, after all, Yvon didn't have much will. And those are the innocent people."

Nancy put the mug on the table and threw her head back to look at the ceiling, where the plaster was mottled; then she looked at Cyriac and asked, "His mother really wanted him to be happy with me?"

"When he began to leave right after church to get back to Boston, she guessed it was because of a girl, and, I'll tell you, this made her happy for him. And she'd smile and even joke a little with him, saying, 'A bouquet of flowers is always a nice gift,' and she'd touch him on the cheek and she'd say, 'I do, I do want you to be happy.' And, going off, he was happy."

Nancy pressed her hands to her face.

"He didn't finish in college, you know," Cyriac said.

Lowering her hands, Nancy said, "I didn't know."

"He thought that he wouldn't be able to make it, that he wasn't good enough, or rich enough, or from an old Yankee family, because the Yankees took over everything from us."

"What do you mean?"

"What do I mean? Well, I can say a lot, because I know a lot about our history, our Franco history. Yes, I do. You have to go back far for me to tell you what I mean. You have to go back to when the French had almost all of North America. I mean, do you know what la Nouvelle France was? I'll tell you. La Nouvelle France was almost all of the North of America. Who do you think founded the cities of Detroit, Des Moines, Du Bois, well, the French did, and, too, all along the Mississippi River? Who do you think the explorers were? La Salle, Marquette, even the Jesuit missionaries, they were French. I'm telling you. The French were here before the Yankees. And then the Yankees came, and they went to war. They fought the French and the Indians, too, who were on the side of the French, because the French made friends with the Indians, even married squaws, yes, and French women married Indian braves. My grandmother, Ma's mother, she was Indian, Micmac. But the Yankees, they defeated the French, and they took over, and here we are, still defeated. It riles me up, it does, and I don't like being riled up, I need to be calm, because what can I do? I'll tell you, Ma was condemned—and yes, I'll say it—by history that she didn't even know anything about, because none of us does, none of us Francos in America knows about our history. You ask a Franco, what do you know about the French General Montcalm defeated by the English General

Wolfe in Quebec, there on the Plains of Abraham? and you get a look, like what? or, what does it matter? and, as a matter of fact, that's when us Francos lost all of North America. I read about it, I learned about it, and here I am, and maybe, yes, I put too much on it, our history. It's like our history isn't even American history. That's what I think. And you've got to think about Yvon, that he was a Franco."

Nancy now pressed her hands against her bosom as though to protect herself.

Cyriac, riled up, said, "You knew Yvon, but you didn't know him. Well, I'm going to tell you more about us Francos. I don't think you know about us, and maybe it isn't very interesting, but I'll tell you, because Yvon was, yes, Franco." Cyriac leaned forward to speak as if he had heard the words from others, over and over, and was repeating them to someone he urgently wanted to know what he had to say, which no one else knew, and here was someone who had to listen to him. "You leave the farm in Canada because it's bankrupt and you come to the States to work in a textile factory, and you wear your Sunday clothes because now you've got work. And I'll tell you something else about us Francos: we take the worst jobs, the job sorting out the pelts, the dirty sheep's bloody pelts, in the sorting room, and we take the jobs that no one else will take because that's the way we are, we'll do what no one else will do. Do you want me to show you the pelt that's been in the closet since my grandfather took it from the mill, a beautiful pelt, maybe that he stole, so we kept it hid away all these years?"

"Show it to me."

Cyriac opened the door to the closet, from where there

came the smell of a cellar, and he brought the thick pelt out to hold it up for Nancy, and when he said, "Feel it, feel it deep," she ran her fingers deep into the yellowish wool; then he hung it back up and, at the table, moved his cup from side to side, thinking.

"Well, to know what we really are, Francos that we are, you got to see us in a small graveyard, all of us standing around an open grave and watching the coffin lowered in the grave, and all with the feeling that we're all being lowered into the grave, all of us together. And you got to see that with snow falling, always with snow falling. It's our history, and no one is interested in our history."

"No," Nancy said, and she meant that if no one else was interested she was, but Cyriac understood her to agree with him, and he said, "No, you see, no one," and Nancy was too tired to try to show she was interested; she was, but perhaps she wasn't, and Cyriac seemed to accept that she wasn't, that no one was.

He said, "Other people count, yes, the black people count, the Irish people count, and the Italian people, and the Polish people, and, oh yes, the Jewish people count, but Francos, they don't count, and because Yvon was a Franco, and because Francos don't count, Yvon was the most American person you could ever want to meet."

This made Nancy become very still.

Again, Cyriac asked if she would like more tea, and now she said she would, and thanked him when he put an unused tea bag in her mug and heated the water to boiling and poured it into the mug, she shaking her head no to milk and sugar. She said, "Can you tell me what had happened to Yvon after he came back from New York?"

He held back for a moment, and she saw in his eyes his animated thinking, then Cyriac said, "Well, Yvon was with you in New York, and Ma said to me that when Yvon came home she'd tell him he had his own life now, so he didn't have to come every Sunday to be with her and go to Mass with her. It was like she was getting ready for him to come back, and she'd show him how she could be strong. She'd make a fist and say, 'I can use my will power, I can, and I don't need Yvon anymore. He's happy now, and that's all I wanted.' She said that."

"Yes," Nancy said.

"But when Yvon came home after going to New York, there he was standing at the door with his valise maybe waiting for Ma to say something to him, but Ma turned away from him and she pressed her forehead to the wall and she hit her head against the wall, and then she turned back to Yvon and she said, 'I'm sorry,' and she said, 'I can't,' and Yvon said, 'I know you can't,' and Yvon put down his valise and went to her and held Ma in his arms. Ma was not a mother who held her sons or let her sons hold her. And, I'll tell you, I couldn't hardly see them for the tears in my eyes, Ma and Yvon there, and me knowing that something happened to them there, and that Ma gave up trying, and that Yvon gave up trying, and why they were holding each other was because they both gave up. And when Ma kissed Yvon on his cheek, he let her go and she let him go, and she went to her room and shut the door. I made tea for Yvon, and we sat at this table and we didn't say anything. And that was all, but it was like everything."

"Yes," Nancy said quietly.

"Let me tell you, I'm not religious, but I can live good

in the world, because I know what happens to you in the world, you live in the dark down here below and you suffer the way the world is, and if you know that, you know how to live in this world. Yvon, he never learned to live in the world the way the world is, and maybe that's strange because even when we were kids out playing he'd say, 'Wow, look at that,' and, 'Wow, wow,' and I'd wonder what made him think that a rock ledge from, oh, all the way back to the ice age was, like, wow, because it was only rock to me, but to him it was wow. I did sometimes understand that what he wanted was so big, so much everything, that for him it had to be as big as all of God. Did he believe? It don't matter, not for Yvon, and, maybe, now not for anybody. And maybe, you know, the best way to hope for everything you want, what only God can give you, is just to long for it even if you don't believe, because for Yvon longing was belief enough, and there was so much longing in him, so much. Even if Yvon knew that there wasn't no God, knew that even when he went to Mass with Ma God was not going to help because there was no God to help—well, if you know that, and still you want to believe, but you can't believe because there is nothing to believe in, that's suffering you can't live with. Yvon wanted to believe, he wanted that more than anything else, and I could tell how much he suffered what he could never ever have, not in this world, and not in any other world. I wouldn't be surprised if Yvon, if he isn't dead, no, not dead, is still wandering around America, oh, all of America, searching for rocks no one ever heard of. Or maybe he became a monk at some monastery and has no contact with this world, even with me."

"Yes," Nancy repeated.

"You know, after he came back from New York, he stayed, though I told him, over and over, to go, but he stayed. Well, Yvon and Ma, they didn't go to Mass on Sunday anymore. Ma, she stayed in her room, the door shut. Yvon went out for a lot of the day and one day when he came in he asked, 'Where's Ma?' and I said, 'In her room,' and I followed him and he stopped at the shut door, but then he opened it, and the room was dark because she'd pulled the shade down and he switched on the light, and I heard him shout, 'Ma,' and I saw that Ma was on her bed. She was shaking bad, her eyes open and staring like she was scared. Yvon lifted her from the bed and a knife fell from her hand and blood burst from her neck onto Yvon's face and his shirt and pants, and she died. He was shivering so much as he put her back on her bed and he knelt by the bed and he leaned his forehead on the edge, and he cried out, 'Ma, Ma, Ma.' I closed Ma's eyes."

Cyriac grasped his chin and held it tight, then he slowly released it.

"I closed her eyes and I put my hands under Yvon's arms and I lifted him up—I remember that a chair by the bed fell over—and I held him, held him while he cried, cried and cried, my brother, the brother I loved, the brother I would do anything for, anything, and I was—I don't know why— calm."

Nancy, too, all at once felt calm, and she too didn't know why; she became still. She said, "And then he came to me."

"I wanted him to go to you. He went to you before I called the police. I washed his face and I buttoned him into his raincoat that was too big for him, and I drove him to the train station and bought him a ticket and I made sure he got on the train."

Nancy said, "I wanted so much to save him, but I couldn't."

"Well, you had to save yourself."

"Oh, save myself—from what?"

Cyriac looked out of the window, and she did also to see that snow was falling among the black bare branches of a large maple tree.

Cyriac said, "From everything."

Nancy watched the snow settling on the branches of the tree.

"Were you brought up with any religion?" Cyriac asked.

"None," she answered quickly.

"Yvon said that you're Jewish. I never met a Jewish person before. You don't practice your Jewish religion?"

"No." She smeared the tears across her face with her fingers and she said, "I loved him, I loved Yvon. That was my religion."

Cyriac raised the back of his hand to his forehead.

Nancy had nothing to save in herself, but she should have been able to save Yvon. Yvon had it in him—she knew he had had it in him—to see all the wonders of the world, and if she had encouraged him in his wonders he would have lived for them.

She said, "Yes, it was in him, it was in Yvon, yes, to shout out, 'Wow,'" and then she fell back into her chair and sobbed.

Cyriac gave her his wrinkled handkerchief, which he

said was clean, and he sat still across the table from her and let her sob, the handkerchief to her face.

Yes, Yvon loved the world, trees, and rain, and rocks. He loved everything. But he failed, failed again and again, because everything was all too far beyond him and he couldn't go any further than where his love got him; and he let go and gave in to some longing that was always there and always greater and greater, some wild longing, and maybe that was still his great, wild, beatific longing, somewhere out far in uncontrollable America.

And Nancy felt something let go in her.

At last she said, "I'm very tired."

"Do you want to sleep for a while?" he asked.

"Sleep where?"

"Follow me," he said, and he led her into a cold bedroom with faded red roses on blue wallpaper. He turned on the radiator.

A glass-fronted cabinet stood against a wall. Nancy went to examine, in neat rows, Yvon's rock collection, a label in capital letters written in ink identifying each and where each was found:

PHLOGOPITE (New Jersey) ILMENITE (Massachusetts) MUCOVITE (New Mexico) MOLYBDENITE (Colorado) PYRRHOTITE (Tennessee) MARCASITE (Kansas) RHODOCHROSITE (Montana) DOLOMITE (Mississippi) ORTHOCLASE (California) HALITE (New York) BARITE (South Dakota) RUTILE (Georgia) ARAGONITE (Arizona) PYRMORPHITE (Idaho) TEMOLITE (Connecticut) CORUNDUM (Pennsylvania) ANDALUSITE (California) VESUVIANTE (Montana) EPIDOTE (Alaska)

BERYL (North Carolina) CHROMITE (Oregon) COPPER (Michigan)

Only the label remained of the quartz that Yvon had given to her, found in Rhode Island.

Nancy pressed her forehead against the glass of the cabinet. The collection would always remain incomplete, because of course all collections were incomplete, some essential element was always missing. Now lost, the quartz, which at the time Yvon had given it to her had meant little to her, and afterward had meant even less because she had forgotten about it, now meant everything, and that meaning, like the rock, was lost. Like the fragment of meteorite. A small heave of breath rose in her, the last impulse of her sobbing, and she drew back from the cabinet.

Cyriac had pulled the spread off the bed and turned the bedclothes down.

"Is this Yvon's bed?" Nancy asked.

"It is," he answered.

Hanging over the bed was a crucifix, the body dull golden against the wood.

"I once knew a Jew who converted to Catholicism," Nancy said. "He had a crucifix in his room. He became a monk."

"Get into bed," Cyriac said.

She took off her shoes and lay down on the bed, and she let Cyriac cover her with the bedclothes. Then he went to the window and for a moment looked out as if searching for something or someone, and she saw, past him, that snow was falling more heavily in the evening dusk. She turned on her side and pressed her face into the pillow as Cyriac drew the blind down to dim the room.

"Go on and sleep—I won't wake you," Cyriac said, and he left the room.

Awake, she stared into the deepening dark; the more she stared the more the dark appeared to her with sudden, odd shifts to deepen, and the more it deepened the more she felt that someone was out there, and this someone might appear, and she waited for him. The waiting was familiar to her, as if she had waited in the same way since before she could remember.

Acknowledgments

My thanks to Joseph Olshan are great for asking me if I was working on a novel, for reading, for making suggestions for linking scenes that make him, I like to think, as much the author as I am, and for seeing the novel through all its stages.

My life is filled with coincidences, and one I am particularly fond of is that the splendid copyeditor of this novel has the nonfictional name of Nancy Green, to whom all thanks.

And many thanks to everyone at Delphinium.

A NOTE ON THE TYPE

This book was set in Walbaum, a typeface designed in 1810 by German punch cutter J.E. Walbaum. Walbaum's type is more French than German in appearance. Like Bodoni, it is a classical typeface, yet its openness and slight irregularities give it a human, romantic quality.

About the author

David Plante grew up in Providence, Rhode Island, within a French-Canadian parish that was palisaded by its language, a French that dated from the time of the first French colonists in the early 17th century in what was then most of North America, La Nouvelle France. His background is very similar to that of Jack Kerouac, who was brought up in a French-speaking parish in Lowell, Massachusetts. Plante has been inspired to write novels rooted in La Nouvelle France, most notably in *The Family*, a contender for the National Book Award. His renowned book, *Difficult Women*, a nonfiction work that profiled Jean Rhys, Sonia Orwell and Germaine Greer, was reissued by The New York Review of Books Press in 2017. He has dual nationality, American and British, but lives in Lucca, Italy.